# The Lookout Tree

D1225795

# The Lookout Tree

A Family's Escape from
the Acadian Deportation

DIANE CARMEL LÉGER

Illustrations by MICHEL LÉGER

NIMBUS
PUBLISHING
—— NIMBUS.CA ——

Nimbus Publishing Limited
3660 Strawberry Hill Street, Halifax, NS, B3K 5A9
(902) 455-4286 nimbus.ca

Printed and bound in Canada

NB1499

**MIX**
Paper from responsible sources
FSC
www.fsc.org    FSC® C013916

Cover illustration: Réjean Roy
Editor: Penelope Jackson
Interior design: Jenn Embree

Text copyright © 2004, 2008, 2009, 2012, 2015, 2019 Diane Carmel Léger
Previously published in French as *La butte à Pétard* by Bouton d'Or Acadie and by Les Éditions d'Acadie in 1989 (three editions)

Library and Archives Canada Cataloguing in Publication
Title: The lookout tree : a family's escape from the Acadian deportation / Diane Carmel Léger.
Other titles: Butte à Pétard. English
Names: Léger, Diane Carmel, 1957- author.
Description: Translation of: La butte à Pétard.
Identifiers: Canadiana 20190120770 | ISBN 9781771087803 (softcover)
Classification: LCC PS8573.E46149 B8813 2019 | DDC jC843/.54—dc23

Nimbus Publishing acknowledges the financial support for its publishing activities from the Government of Canada, the Canada Council for the Arts, and from the Province of Nova Scotia. We are pleased to work in partnership with the Province of Nova Scotia to develop and promote our creative industries for the benefit of all Nova Scotians.

*In memory of my dear father,*
*Raymond à Elphège à Arthur*
*à Marcellin à Jean à Charles*
*à Jacques à Jacques à Jacques*

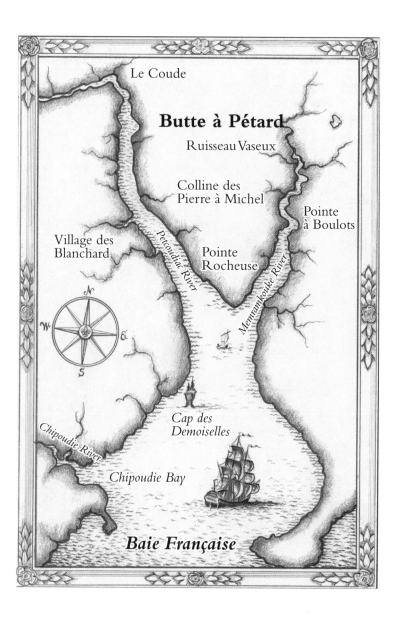

# Contents

# Author's Note

*Founded as a French colony in 1604, Acadia was attacked and* changed hands several times when conflicts arose between France and England. The Acadians, who were mostly farmers, did not wish to bear arms against France or England. Whether under control of the French or English authorities, the Acadians had managed to live in peace and harmony with the Mi'kmaq since 1604. Had they taken up arms against the French soldiers, they would have been fighting against their Acadian relatives in French territories such as Île Saint-Jean (Prince Edward Island) and Île Royale (Cape Breton Island).

Acadians were declared French Neutrals after the Treaty of Utrecht in 1713, and they continued a prosperous existence as British subjects until 1755. That was the year Charles Lawrence, Nova Scotia's new lieutenant-governor, decided to deport them and confiscate their farmland, homes, and cattle for future English settlers. The Acadian Deportation lasted several years. Acadians called this period and subsequent relocations *le Grand Dérangement*, the Great Upheaval.

The majority of Acadians were forced aboard over-crowded ships and deported to the Thirteen Colonies (later the United States), where they were not welcome and endured great hardship. Hundreds died aboard the vessels or drowned. Families were separated, never to see each other again.

In 1755, there were roughly fourteen thousand inhabitants of French origin in Acadia. Of these, approximately ten thousand were deported. The rest fled to New France or hid in the forest, often with help from the Mi'kmaq.

This account of a fictional family represents the many real families who sought refuge in the forests of Acadia. Most of the Acadians in the Maritimes today are their descendants.

For this story, I changed the month of the burning of the hamlet of la Butte-à-Pétard. Only a small part of the Memramcook Valley was burned at the beginning of September 1755. In November of that year, the British were ordered to set fire to the rest of Memramcook, including la Butte-à-Pétard.

During this period, the Mi'kmaq still lived a nomadic life as they had for thousands of years. Some camped very close to the Acadian settlements, which might explain why the French spoken by the Acadians was enriched with words from the Mi'kmaw language.

According to oral history, the Mi'kmaq warned the people of Memramcook about the British scheme to remove them. There were three known hideouts in the woods of Memramcook, and one of them was near la Butte-à-Pétard.

All of the characters are imaginary, except for Lawrence, Boishébert, Beausoleil, and a Cyr nicknamed "Pétard." Oral history portrays Pétard as audacious and a bit of a braggart who was fond of Mi'kmaw customs.

SUMMER 1755

# LE GRAND DÉRANGEMENT

## CHAPTER 1

# Fidèle's Mission

*Eleven-year-old Fidèle paddles down the winding* Memramkouke River. His father has entrusted him with an important task. He must find Kitpou, a Mi'kmaw man who may have the latest news since the British capture of Fort Beauséjour. Has war broken out again between France and England after forty years of peace?

The waves grow larger as Fidèle nears Chipoudie Bay, where the Memramkouke River meets the Petcoudiac River. Near la Pointe Rocheuse, the wigwams appear to have been abandoned. Have the Mi'kmaq changed campsites here as they did at la Butte-à-Pétard?

Fidèle notices a thin line of glistening mud on the shore. *The tide is going out*, he thinks. *I should be going back.* The tide falls very quickly in this part of Acadie. Twice a day, the rivers of the Baie Française drain to almost a trickle. One must know them well before venturing out in a canoe. Wisely, Fidèle turns the canoe around.

"Fidèle!"

The boy turns to see a canoe rounding the rocky point. It is Kitpou! Fidèle, relieved and pleased with himself, breaks into a wide grin. Now he can get the news his father wants. He paddles towards Kitpou, but his relief turns to fear upon hearing his friend's words.

"The Redcoats are capturing Acadians!" shouts Kitpou. "More ships are anchored at Fort Lawrence and Beauséjour! They could be here as soon as tomorrow!"

Kitpou points to the river and says, "You warn them on the Memramkouke! I'll warn them on the Petcoudiac!" Then, with great strokes, he turns back.

The boy's heart beats faster than ever as he paddles with all his strength. This is not the news Acadians expected. Soldiers are not just fighting soldiers anymore. This time, British soldiers are after Acadians! Will he be able to warn all of the Acadian families along the crooked river, with its many twists and turns slowing him down?

With fear fuelling a newfound strength, Fidèle continues on the Memramkouke. Just past la Pointe-à-Boulots, he shouts to some farmers baling hay in the marsh.

"The Redcoats are coming to capture us!"

The men wave back and run toward their farms. One of them heads toward the church to ring the bell. Fidèle will not need to alert anyone for some distance.

He is able to reach the riverside just below his village before the muddy riverbed stops his canoe. Fidèle warns more Acadians in the marshes as he runs home to la Butte-à-Pétard.

He wishes he could run as fast as his mind is racing.

*What is going to happen to Acadians? How can they escape? Farmers can't fight soldiers! There are way more children than adults! Little children can't run fast. And they are noisy and cry a lot when they are scared.* Mon Dieu! *What about Maman, who will be having her baby soon? Babies cry all the time!*

His heart beats quickly. With a sudden burst of strength, Fidèle runs faster. Tears fly from his cheeks. *Papa will know what to do*, he keeps reminding himself.

Meanwhile, in the upper marshes of the Memramkouke Valley, Fidèle's father, Jacques; his grandfather, nicknamed Pétard; and their neighbours have finished baling the hay. After a long day's work, they head toward their thatched-roof houses for a hearty supper.

Jacques teases his father, Pétard: "Will you be having supper with the widow Rosalie this evening?"

Pétard answers with a grin, "I sure would like to, but I'm afraid she would slam the door in my face! She's no delicate rose, that Rosalie." He bursts into his very peculiar laugh: "Cla! Cla! Cla!"

Above the laughter, Jacques and the men hear someone calling faintly: "Papa! Papa!"

Jacques turns and sees his son running towards them across the marsh. Fidèle is clearly distressed and worn out from running. Jacques runs towards his son and the men follow.

When he reaches his father, a breathless Fidèle manages to say, "Soldiers are coming to get us, Papa! Maybe tomorrow…Kitpou warning Petcoudiac…Me, Memramkouke…Upper farms don't know…."

"Mon Dieu!" cries out Jacques. He embraces his son and says, "You've done well, Fidèle. Someone else will run to the upper farms." To the others he says, "The rumours were true! The Redcoats are after all of us!

"I knew not to trust that devil Lawrence!" yells Pétard, livid. "Even the English in Halifax don't like him! That wolf has been planning all along to get rid of Acadians and steal our farmland!"

Some men swear and others wail.

Jacques sends a volunteer to the next hamlet and Pétard yells to the young man, "Just tell Ti-Pruce. He can warn the rest of his neighbours at La Montain!"

A few men start to panic. "There must be a misunderstanding. A lieutenant-governor can't do that to his own British subjects, let alone our families here in French Territory. We're not criminals!"

One shouts, "Lawrence waited for harvest time so that the British soldiers could take as much as possible from us!" Another adds, "After living with them peacefully and feeding their soldiers for forty-two years!" More swearing.

A man laments, "If we flee, our families will be hunted like animals."

Another cries, "Oh non! Mon Dieu! Such cruelty to innocent women and children!"

Pétard tries to calm them. "Listen, men! We're lucky that we have enough time to set up a good hiding place up the muddy stream. The sooner we leave, the better."

Not having much choice, the men nod in agreement.

Pétard turns to his son and asks, "Jacques, what are you going to do?"

"The midwife was by this morning. She said Marie will be giving birth this evening and must stay in bed, or she'll die in childbirth. Marie and I will remain here until the child is born. I don't want to risk losing her or the child. We've been through this before without a midwife. Don't worry. We'll join you before morning."

The men rush home, dreading to tell their families the terrible reason for their escape to the woods.

The people of the Memramkouke Valley cannot believe they must leave their homes. The men and women brace themselves to be very strong for their children's sake, knowing that this night and the ones that follow will be very difficult.

## CHAPTER 2
# The Hiding Place

*At home they quickly prepare to flee to the woods. Prémélia,* Fidèle's twelve-year-old sister, grabs a few pewter bowls and goblets and throws them into a bag. Next, she unhooks the little cooking pot and puts a handful of candles inside. At the cupboard, she fills three small bags: one with millet, one with oats, and one with wheat flour. In her haste, she drops flour on the floor, near her mother's bed.

"Leave it, *chère,*" says her mother, Marie, in a weak voice.

"Maman, should I bring butter and meat?"

"Not in this heat. You'll not be able to keep it fresh and away from the animals. Don't forget a needle and thread and some cloth for mending."

Prémélia places everything but the pot in the middle of a sturdy piece of cloth and ties the ends together to make a big bundle.

"Maman, I don't want to leave you."

"Don't be scared, chère. I've been through child-birth before and it's best that I not be moved right now. The birth pains have already begun. It won't be long. Your father and I will join you before morning."

In their garden, Fidèle and his grandfather hastily pull out potatoes, onions, and carrots and toss them into a bag. Pétard tells Fidèle, "It's like my father would have said: 'King Louis doesn't eat better vegetables than ours.' The neighbours are so jealous of our big potatoes. Cla! Cla!"

"Pépère, is the bag full enough now?"

"Yes, but I see a gap."

"A gap?"

"Yes, just room enough for a little jug of spruce beer to fit in nicely. It is medicinal, you know."

Coming from the barn, Jacques hears his father and smiles despite the circumstances. Near Fidèle, he puts down a big knife, an axe, some rope, three bows, and several arrows.

"Will we be in hiding for long, Papa?"

"I don't know, son," says Jacques, putting a hand on Fidèle's shoulder. "A few weeks, maybe longer. I hope the British will come to their senses before the cold weather. But with you such a good little hunter and trapper, we won't starve."

"Please let me stay with you and Maman. I could help defend us against those red devils!" begs Fidèle.

Jacques looks at his son, whose temperament is so much like Pétard's.

"Fidèle, be reasonable. Acadians are farmers, not soldiers. Since Queen Anne's reign of England, our family and neighbours have kept their promise to not take up arms against either the French or the English. This isn't our war. It'll soon be over like the others. Your mother and I will join you before the British soldiers arrive."

The boy bows his head, and Jacques hugs his son tenderly. They walk home.

Wanting to join them, the grandfather rushes from the root cellar. His jug slips from his hands and smashes on the ground, splashing foamy spruce beer on his breeches.

"Darn jug! If you want to slip away from my hands, then I don't need you!"

Jacques and Fidèle, grinning at Pétard's antics, wait for him before entering the house. They join Prémélia at the table for a quick meal of *fricot* and fresh bread. They say a supper prayer together.

Not long after, the neighbours gather in front of Jacques's house. They wait patiently outside as the two children and their grandfather say goodbye to Jacques and Marie.

At Marie's bedside, the children and Pétard take turns to hug her gently.

"Be brave and pray this evening. I'll see you… later," she tells them.

Worried about their mother, who is obviously in pain, Prémélia and Fidèle can only nod.

Marie looks at Pétard and smiles feebly.

"You take care of yourself and your grandchildren. I know that the widow Rosalie will be there, so try not to be *escrable* by teasing her.

"Cla! Cla!" laughs Pétard half-heartedly.

On the threshold, it is Jacques's turn to hug the children goodnight.

"Join us as quickly as possible, son," whispers Pétard gravely.

With their bundles of provisions, they join the other families and leave for the muddy stream. At the edge of the woods, in the soft light of dusk, Prémélia and Fidèle turn to look at their home one last time.

Against the lovely pink and purple sky, the grim-faced villagers move in a column toward the dark outline of the forest. The murmur of desperate prayers permeates the peaceful forest.

**CHAPTER 3**

# The Raven

*The next morning, there is much concern for Jacques and Marie,* who have yet to arrive at the hiding place. No one can risk the safety of the group to look for them. Prémélia and Fidèle are very anxious about their parents. They busy themselves helping their grandfather build a primitive shelter like the others.

The lean-tos are tiny and damp with morning dew. The beds are made of small stacks of fir branches. No cooking fire will be made, because the smoke might alert the soldiers.

By early afternoon, Jacques and Marie have still not arrived. What went wrong? Was it a difficult birth? Did the soldiers come already? Fidèle can wait no longer. As he slinks away from the group, Prémélia stops him.

"No, Fidèle. You risk getting captured by the soldiers and endangering everyone."

Frustrated at being caught, the boy kicks some stones. His older sister tries to comfort him. "I'm very worried about Maman and Papa, too. I hope they are hiding somewhere. They would want us to stay safe and pray for them now."

But Fidèle can't pray right now. He's too upset about his parents. How can the rest of them, especially his grandfather, stay there and do nothing? As soon as he can, Fidèle sneaks away from the campsite without being seen.

Near the edge of the woods, he smells smoke! He scrambles up a big beech tree. His heart leaps at the loathsome scene before him on la Butte-à-Pétard. Homes and barns are engulfed in flames. Soldiers are everywhere—trampling gardens, leading cattle away, and seizing other farm animals. Where are his parents?

There is no sign of anyone but the Redcoats. Like a swarm of devils, they are setting fire to the entire village. Fidèle trembles. *What did we do to deserve this? Have the soldiers captured my parents? What will they do to them? Could Maman and Papa be hiding nearby?*

Before he can think any further, Fidèle hears some strange words and sees three Redcoats beneath his tree. He freezes, terrified, certain they are going to look up and see him. At that instant, the men raise their muskets but aim in another direction. Fidèle looks to where the guns are pointing and sees a Mi'kmaw woman.

She doesn't look like the other Mi'kmaw women Fidèle knows. She has a sinister air about her, almost

ghostly. She is draped in a strange, shiny cloak of black feathers, with more raven feathers strewn throughout her long, flowing hair. Fearlessly, she faces the soldiers' muskets. *Who is she and where did she come from? Why is she just standing there?*

The soldiers fire, but their musket balls do not seem to harm the woman facing them. Is she a witch? A spirit? The soldiers fire again. This time she starts floating toward them. Frightened, the soldiers run back to the village.

His heart hammering in his chest, Fidèle climbs down the tree. He hears a loud caw but cannot see a bird nor the woman. She has vanished. Fidèle runs as fast as he can to the hiding place.

At the woodland refuge, the sky is beginning to darken with smoke from the village. The families are horrified. And Fidèle is missing!

At last, the boy appears and confirms their fears that their homes were set on fire, telling them that three soldiers were near the hiding place.

"Did you see your parents?" asks Pétard anxiously.

"No, Pépère!" he cries in anguish.

"The Redcoats may have already figured out that we are upstream," says a neighbour. "Perhaps the three soldiers went for reinforcements."

"We must hide deeper in the woods, toward the Petcoudiac River, before they come back!" insists another man.

All the men agree except for Pétard, who declares, "I'm staying here with my grandchildren to wait for Jacques and Marie."

The rest of the families prepare for their next move. Before they leave, Kitpou arrives unexpectedly to report that some Acadians have fled to New France, Île Saint-Jean, and Île Royale. He pauses before revealing the worst news: Mi'kmaq have seen hundreds of Acadians, young and old, imprisoned at nearby Fort Beauséjour and Fort Lawrence. He then looks toward Pétard and his grandchildren.

"The soldiers came just after sunrise. Jacques, Marie, and the newborn were forced aboard the ship heading to the forts."

## CHAPTER 4
# The Petcoudiac

*With the shock of Jacques and Marie's capture, Pétard, Prémélia,* and Fidèle decide to join the others in their flight toward the Petcoudiac. Kitpou leads the group. They smell smoke as they approach their destination. The adults glance at each other despairingly and stop walking. When a cloud of smoke appears overhead, the children understand why they have stopped. Apparently, more soldiers have set fire to Acadian settlements along the Petcoudiac River. The fugitives are trapped in the woods, between the two rivers and the fires. Some slump to the ground and others wail in despair, not caring if marauding soldiers might hear them.

Away from the group, Kitpou and the Acadian men sit on a carpet of moss. They must decide where to go. Is there a safe place in Acadie, or will they have to leave the colony?

For Pétard, the decision to leave the area is much harder because of Jacques and Marie's imprisonment at the nearby forts. Fidèle, who has been eavesdropping on the meeting, interrupts his grandfather.

"Pépère, where would Papa and Maman go if they were to escape?"

Pétard is so overwhelmed with sorrow that, for once, he is at a loss for words.

"Escape the fort…?" the old man repeats, slowly. He places his weathered hand on his grandson's shoulder. "You're right." Pétard straightens up and signals for Prémélia to join them.

"Children, we mustn't give up hope and leave our land. *Sapristi*! Our family will stay here and wait for Jacques, Marie, and the baby. Yes, Fidèle, you're absolutely right. We must wait for them near la Butte, where they can easily find us."

Prémélia and Fidèle are relieved that they will stay less than a day's walk from their imprisoned parents. The others decide to leave the area by taking the forest trail to Cocagne and continuing to the safety of the faraway Miramichi River.

"Your decision is a wise one for you," approves Pétard. "But my grandchildren and I will return to the hiding place of the muddy stream. My Jacques may escape the fort and find us. Don't worry about us. We'll be fine. A small group of people has a better chance at surviving and going undetected by the soldiers."

Everyone respects his decision, for Pétard is known for his cleverness and audacity, as well as the skills that he has learned from the Mi'kmaq.

"Would another person be too many?" inquires the widow Rosalie.

All heads turn toward the stout woman.

"My beautiful house in Beaubassin was set on fire five years ago, and now Redcoats have burned down my new home. I've had enough! I don't want to start over again in a different place. I'd rather wait here until it dawns on the British soldiers just who has been feeding them all these years."

"For your lovely presence, Madame, there will surely be a place in my hut," teases Pétard. "Besides, you make darn good fricot for a woman from Beaubassin. Cla! Cla!"

"Well, you're going to need a whole lot of soup. You're as skinny as a broomstick!" Rosalie retorts, causing some to smile.

In the late afternoon, Pétard's group bids farewell to their neighbours.

"*Adieu!* When this is all over, you will come back to dance on la Butte and eat fricot to celebrate my marriage to Rosalie!"

"Me, your wife? Never in your life!" the widow protests.

Secretly, Pétard and Rosalie are pleased to have made a few villagers chuckle before their sad departure.

The two children say goodbye to their friends and neighbours. After the last person disappears among the fir trees, they sit down under a wild cherry tree. They are suddenly alone, and with their bewilderment comes more fear. Their parents, their home, and their village and its people are really gone. Now they are only two children with two old people. Will they be able to survive in the woods so close to danger? Will the rest of the family escape the fort?

Fidèle looks at his big sister and says, "Lia, I don't know if staying is the right choice anymore."

Prémélia tries to comfort him. "I think it's best to stay. I'm sure that Kitpou will visit once in a while. Rosalie is strong as an ox and Pépère is sly as a fox. You hunt as well as Papa. As for me, Maman said that I know the medicinal herbs as well as she does. I'll teach you what I know about plants, and you can teach me to hunt. We'll manage until Maman and Papa come home."

Pétard and Kitpou make a temporary shelter while the others cut evergreen branches to sleep on.

Late that night, they sit around a small fire and sip spruce tea.

"Pépère, how many days are we going to stay here before going back to the muddy stream?" asks Fidèle.

"One week. Enough time to make sure that the soldiers have moved on."

"What if the soldiers come back?"

"Don't worry about them, Fidèle. Kitpou is going to help us build a better hideout, and I still have a few more tricks."

Prémélia is fretful. "But Papa won't be able to find us if we're so well hidden."

"Your father will find us. He's a Pétard, is he not? Cla! Cla!"

Kitpou tosses a few sticks on the fire and sits down between the youngsters. Everyone stares silently at the flames. In his mind, Fidèle sifts through the day's events: Redcoats crawling like red ants all over his grandfather's hill, some setting fire to the houses and barns, others stealing the animals and raiding the gardens. Then the three soldiers beneath the lookout tree…and the black-feathered woman! He forgot to tell the others about her!

Fidèle recounts his sighting of the fearless Mi'kmaw woman who drove away the three soldiers.

"Are you certain they fired at her?"

"Yes, Pépère."

"Kitpou, what does the sudden appearance of a Mi'kmaw spirit clothed in black feathers mean? Who is she?"

"That spirit, who was once a *bouhine,* could be here to help or to harm. A bouhine is a Mi'kmaw man or woman who possesses extraordinary powers. But this one is the spirit of an unknown bouhine who has not been among my people for very long. The few who have seen her say that she only appears during the flow of the *refoul*, and she sometimes chooses the shape of a bird."

The youngsters and Rosalie are shaken by yet another danger added to their ordeal.

"Don't fear the bouhine. I've never heard of a Mi'kmaw spirit harming Acadians. It's time to sleep," reassures Pétard.

But no one can find sleep for many hours, and when they do, their nightmares are terrifying.

They spend a week there, cautiously hunting for food by day and desperately trying to comfort each other by night. All are reeling from the abrupt change in their lives and from the cruelty of the British taking away their parents—except for Kitpou. He is used to the British authorities' mistreatment of his people and is unsurprised by their actions.

The Acadians try to be brave. In their sleep, the children cry out for their parents. Finally, the seventh day dawns, and they pack their meagre belongings once again and prepare to return to their first hideout. There is no sign of soldiers, and no sign of Jacques and Marie.

Kitpou leads the way. At a clearing atop a ridge, he pauses. From there, they can take one last look at the brown Petcoudiac River before retreating into the woods toward la Butte-à-Pétard.

"The refoul is coming," observes Prémélia.

Twice a day, this unique wave rolls in from the Baie Française and up the rivers of the region, a harbinger of the incoming tide. The children and Rosalie shudder, remembering that the refoul heralds not only the incoming tide, but also the bouhine.

AUTUMN 1756

# THE HIDEOUT

CHAPTER 5

# The Feast

*Over the course of a year, Prémélia's predictions have come true.*
Kitpou visits them whenever the Mi'kmaq move to
new hunting grounds or when he is called to scout
for his own people or the French soldiers. During his
stays, they learn how to make moccasins, snowshoes,
and birchbark containers. Fidèle has taught her to snare
rabbits with spruce roots and to bowhunt small game.
She has taught him how to identify and prepare medicinal plants. The youngsters often climb the big beech
tree to check for signs of life near their village and the
surrounding area. To the children's relief, Pétard and
Rosalie show courage and endurance. And somehow,
even on the most difficult days, their grandfather still
finds ways to make them smile.

On this September afternoon, the siblings are
harvesting burdock plants and birchbark for medicine.
After pulling several burdock plants, Fidèle looks down.

"These burrs are a nuisance to pick. I have more on me than on my bag!"

"That's why they're called 'lovers'—because they stick to you. You look like a big *madouesse* with those prickly burrs on your backside!" Prémélia teases.

"I've had enough. Here, you! Stop your mocking and carry your share of these measly lovers! Let's go home."

"Fidèle, we must look for some *mashcoui*, too."

They collect the birchbark on their way back to the hideout. A raven flies overhead and perches on the highest branch of a white pine. Prémélia pauses momentarily to observe the great bird. Fidèle quickens his step.

Meanwhile, Rosalie and Pétard are alone at the wigwam.

"Oh, misery of miseries! I've had enough of living like a hunted animal!"

"Your aches are bothering you still?" Pétard asks.

"Oh, Pétard. It's not only my aches. I just can't go on living in hiding. Not at my age."

Rosalie begins to weep like a little girl. Pétard embraces her.

"You and I made it through the last war between England and France. The English will come to their senses when the *levées* and *aboiteaux* need repairing, or when France gets its next turn to govern Acadie. Rosalie, you're the strongest woman I know, and you're just as stubborn as me…Shh. The children are returning. Try to stop crying, *ma belle.*"

"I'm not your belle," she answers in mock protest, wiping her tears.

The children appear, proudly displaying their harvest.

"Here are some lovers to invigorate you and some mashcoui to soothe your rheumatism, Rosalie," Prémélia announces teasingly.

"Merci. I suppose it can't do me any harm," sniffs Rosalie.

"Are you crying?" Prémélia asks.

"Me? Crying? Rosalie, old Louis's daughter? Not on your life!" insists Rosalie, frowning. She clears her throat.

"Prémélia, fetch some water and boil it. Cut off the burdock roots and save a few burrs. Fidèle, clean those *poulamons* over there. And Pétard, don't look at me like that."

The old man smiles and goes back to repairing the dwelling. He is very proud of his wigwam hidden in a clump of spruce and brush. The cone-shaped hut is made of poles and birchbark covered with balsam branches for warmth and camouflage. The door is a hanging deer hide. The beaten dirt floor is carpeted with fir twigs. At night, smoke from the fire in the central pit filters through the opening at the top of the wigwam.

To avoid being detected by soldiers searching for Acadians returning near la Butte, they gathered the wigwam materials far from the first hiding place. Pétard forbids the children from using the charred remains of their former home as firewood. Should the soldiers return and see the ruins of the village undisturbed and the lean-tos of their first hiding place untouched, they will believe that the fugitives have gone.

When Rosalie leaves to wash her cooking pot in the stream, Pétard takes advantage of time alone with his grandchildren.

"Rosalie's aches and pains have been worse lately. I would like to give her a nice present. A feed of vegetables would certainly cheer her up."

"But Pépère, there aren't any garden vegetables in the forest," objects Prémélia.

"That may be right, but there could be some old vegetables left in last year's gardens."

"But you told us never to set foot on la Butte during the war," reminds Fidèle.

"That's true, but I never forbade *myself* from going back. Cla! Cla! Tomorrow, Fidèle and I will pretend to go hunting. Prémélia, don't say anything to Rosalie. It'll be a big surprise."

The following day, Pétard and his grandson leave, each hiding a large cloth bag in his shirt. At the edge of the forest, Fidèle hands over his bag before climbing the beech tree. From there, he keeps watch as his grandfather cautiously makes his way to where the gardens used to be.

Sorrow overcomes Fidèle. The terrible pain of missing his parents grows stronger as he stares at the ruins of their former home. *Is Maman better? Can a baby survive in a prison? Is Papa able to protect them at Fort Beauséjour?*

His stomach grumbles, reminding him of the food at harvest time. For over a year, he has eaten nothing but wild game, fish, roots, and berries. How good it would be to devour his favourite meal once more: boiled pork with *passe-pierre,* corn on the cob, and fresh bread. And for dessert, blueberry pie with a big dollop of cream.

After a while, Fidèle sees Pétard returning with something in both bags. His proud grin tells Fidèle that he has found some precious vegetables. Pétard opens a bag to show some shrivelled potatoes. He then opens the other bag, showing its fresh parsley and yellowing chives, then puts them in the potato bag.

"I can hardly believe it! Wait till Rosalie sees this!"

"Cla! Cla! Cla! My Rose will love me so much for this that she might not get angry with me for a whole week! My name may be Pétard, but I'm no fool."

"Pépère, Rosalie's hero because of old potatoes! Ha!"

"I've another surprise. The soldiers missed burning an apple tree."

"No! Apples? We're so lucky!"

"You better believe it. The branches are bending to the ground with the weight of the red jewels. Now, you run along to the hideout with the first surprise. I'll fill this bag with apples and join you at the wigwam."

As Fidèle approaches the hideout, he pulls out an old potato and waves it in the air.

Rosalie cries out, "Where did you get that?"

"Pépère gave it to me. This bag is full of potatoes, parsley, and chives from our old garden. And he went back for apples!"

"Apples!" Prémélia exclaims, in disbelief.

"*Saint Esprit*! Pétard risked going back to the village! The old fool!"

"Pépère did it for you, Rosalie. He wanted to cheer you up," says Fidèle.

After a pause, the widow's scowl softens. She mumbles, her eyes filling with tears, "Now, I'm too *bénaise* to get angry at that old braggart."

"Rosalie, you said that you never cry," Prémélia gently remarks.

"This is different," she answers, wiping her eyes. "These are tears of joy."

"Joy, and maybe love?" the girl dares to suggest.

"Prémélia à Jacques à Pétard! What's that you say?" the widow bellows.

"I beg your pardon," offers Prémélia nervously, as Fidèle pokes her with his elbow.

The children try to stifle their giggling as Rosalie, with her hands on her hips, frowns at them, pretending to be angry.

"Now, my escrables, help me surprise Pétard with the grandest feast the old weasel has ever tasted."

All three go about their tasks and, for the first time since they have been in hiding, they begin to hum and then even sing together.

Quite some time later, just when Fidèle is starting to think that Pétard is taking too long, he spots his grandfather at the top of the clearing. "Here's our guest of honour!" shouts Fidèle, jubilant.

Pétard stumbles and collapses to the ground, sending the apples rolling everywhere. "He's hurt!" Prémélia cries out.

"I should have stayed to keep watch at la Butte," wails Fidèle.

"The soldiers have wounded him!" shrieks Rosalie.

She runs to Pétard with the children.

"Oh, *mon cher* Pétard…" cries Rosalie, as she bends over him.

"My big, beautiful Rosalieeeee…" he mumbles before losing consciousness.

"Oh, cher..." moans Rosalie, touching his forehead.

She sniffs the air once and then again near Pétard's open mouth.

"What's that I smell?" Rising to her feet and throwing her hands in the air, she bellows, "He's drunk! The little rat!"

Greatly relieved that their grandfather is not wounded, Fidèle and Prémélia burst into nervous laughter.

"Ah, the drink, the drink! Spruce beer! He's just like my late husband!"

Rosalie stands up and glares down at Pétard, lying with his mouth still wide open. When he starts snoring loudly, the children chuckle.

"Enough," she snaps at them. "It was very foolish and dangerous of your grandfather. Drunk as he is, soldiers could've easily caught him or—"

Fidèle dares to say, "Pépère hasn't drunk anything but spruce tea and water for over a year. He's just not used to beer."

Prémélia says quietly, "You were scared for Pépère, eh, Rosalie?"

For a moment, Rosalie looks like she is going to cry.

"Please forgive him," pleads Prémélia. "Our grandfather isn't a drunkard. Don't worry, there's probably no beer left."

"Ah, that man, that man...your grandfather boasts about being well hidden, but what does he do? He goes to the very top of his hill in full view. He could've been killed!" grumbles Rosalie, looking down at Pétard.

A few hours later, Rosalie and the children are seated before what seems to them a true feast. They eat slowly, savouring each delicious bite. As they are enjoying the meal, Pétard awakens from his slumber. Humbly, he says to them, "Please forgive my foolishness. I found a jug of beer with a few drops left."

"Judging by your triumphant return, monsieur, they must've been mighty big drops!"

Pétard smiles at her sheepishly.

The children try to stifle their giggles once more.

Rosalie clears her throat.

"Still, I suppose I'll forgive you for getting drunk. May it never happen again!" With a little grin, she adds, "And…merci for the best present I've ever received."

Very pleased with himself, Pétard winks at the children.

Prémélia ladles the potato and rabbit stew into a wooden bowl, garnishes it with parsley and chives, and hands it to her grandfather, declaring, "This is the best meal in Acadie, Pépère."

Fidèle says, "There's even warm applesauce for dessert!"

"Well, well, well, I never thought I'd be eating a dessert in hiding. But I'm not quite ready for it yet.

That spruce beer gave me a terrible bellyache. Instead, I'll tell you a good story on this festive occasion."

Feeling the wonderful, warm fullness of eating a delicious meal, the others forget their hardships as they sit around the fire and listen to the old storyteller. By the time the story is finished, Fidèle is asleep and Prémélia is nodding off. Through half-shut eyes, she spies Rosalie giving Pétard a peck on the cheek as she hands him a bowl of stew. This day is the happiest since their forest exile began.

## CHAPTER 6
# The Bluecoats

*After fishing upstream, Prémélia and Fidèle admire the forest* clothed in its bright fall colours. It is a sharp contrast to their faded clothes, which are too small for the growing youngsters. With *nigogs* resting on their shoulders and eels in their baskets, they make their way back to the hideout, very satisfied with their catches.

"Six eels! We're good at fishing," boasts Fidèle.

"Oh, we're quite the fishermen with our nigogs," teases his sister. "We'll have to dry some. I'm going to show you how to attach the eel skins around Pépère's leg so he won't limp so much."

"I told you how Pépère twisted his leg, eh, Lia?"

"Yes, Fidèle. You shouldn't have laughed so much when he fell."

"Prémélia, if only you could've seen him mimicking the time he wrestled the big poulamon who wouldn't let go of the *enfilée*. Pépère was in the middle of imitating the struggling fish, his body wiggling and full cheeks ready to burst, when he twisted his leg and fell flat on his face into the mud. There was even mud in his nostrils! You would have laughed, too! He started laughing himself but had to stop when the mud went into his mouth."

"Wait until you see him with all these eel skins tied around his leg," says his sister. "Then you'll have another funny story to—"

"Shh! Listen!"

They hear nothing but forest sounds. The children stay very still.

"Someone was calling. Maybe from la Butte," says Fidèle quietly. "We should go to the beech tree for a closer look."

"Yes, but we must be very careful."

After ten minutes of walking as soundlessly as possible, they reach the lookout.

As her brother climbs the tree, Prémélia hides a short distance away. Once Fidèle gets la Butte in view, he shouts to his sister, "French soldiers are leaving our village! We must catch up to them before they leave!"

Astonished, Prémélia runs to him.

"Fidèle! Wait! Let me see first," she whispers.

"Hurry, Lia. They're leaving."

Prémélia climbs the lower branches and raises her voice.

"No! They're wearing blue coats! Pépère said French soldiers wear grey coats."

"Capitaine Boishébert wears a blue coat."

"Because he's a captain. Maybe it's just the French officers who wear blue. But all of these soldiers are dressed in blue. They could be helping the Redcoats."

"No, they've got to be French soldiers," insists Fidèle. "Listen again, maybe an officer will yell out more orders."

They hear nothing more. The soldiers retreat in silence.

"French or English, they must be going to Fort Beauséjour," concludes Prémélia.

"No doubt you're right. Oh, Lia, what will happen to Maman and Papa?"

"I'm worried about them too. We must tell Pépère about the soldiers right away."

On their way back to the hideout, they come across their grandfather picking spruce gum. Pétard turns from the tree to tease them, but stops when he hears about the soldiers.

"Sapristi! Bluecoats! They're from Boston. You did well not to approach them. They dislike us even more than the Redcoats! We'll have to stay in the wigwam for at least a few days, in case soldiers come searching around here again."

And so they take refuge in the well-concealed wigwam. Sitting in the dark on a log or reclining on a bough bed is tedious, but it's preferable to the damp and musty prisons of the English forts. They avoid making a fire to cook their meals. Fortunately, they have some dried food stored away. To pass the time, they chew on spruce gum and listen to Pétard's stories.

Fidèle lifts the deerskin door and peers outside.

"At last! The sun is going down!"

Agitated, Fidèle stands to stretch his legs and wonders aloud, "What are those Bluecoats doing at the Redcoats' fort? Do you think that Papa, Maman, and the baby have escaped?"

"Let's pray for them, Fidèle," says Pétard, wearily.

Prémélia murmurs, "The baby was born over a year ago and may be walking by now. Can a baby grow up healthy and learn to walk in prison? I wonder what name Maman and Papa have chosen for him or her."

Pétard looks at his grandchildren and quickly changes the subject.

"Did you know that in order to choose their own name, some young Mi'kmaq undergo a ritual fast in the sweat lodge?" Without waiting for an answer, Pétard continues, "When they leave the lodge, they take the name of the first animal or thing they see. So our friend Kitpou saw an eagle as he left the lodge."

"How strange they are, those savages!" says Rosalie.

Pétard retorts, "Savages? Rosalie! I can't believe an Acadian would ever say such a thing! After all the Mi'kmaq have done for us from the very beginning! Our ancestors wouldn't have survived here without their generosity and skills!" He takes a breath to calm himself. "Rosalie, your anger is misdirected. The Mi'kmaq are our loyal friends. Be angry at the French authorities for ordering the Mi'kmaw soldiers to burn your village so that the British soldiers could not use them during their attacks on Fort Beauséjour. Be angry at the British authorities for savagely removing their own subjects during a time of peace and taking everything from us except the clothes on our back!"

Rosalie bows her head and wipes away a tear with her tattered shawl.

Pétard gently chides her. "Rosalie, we live in a wigwam in the woods. Does that make *us* 'savages'?"

She fails to see any humour, but shakes her head slowly.

Fidèle and Prémélia look away, not wanting to hurt the widow's pride.

"Kitpou should've been here many days ago," says Prémélia after a while. "What could be keeping him?"

"The soldiers must have captured him," concludes Fidèle grimly.

"He may be helping his people. No cause for concern yet," says Pétard.

No one wants to ponder this further, knowing full well the dangers their friend may have encountered in the woods.

At night, they come out of the wigwam, which seems like a prison now. Lethargic, they slowly stretch their limbs and breathe in the night air.

The second day of their confinement, they speak less. To avoid more boredom and worry, they sleep longer.

After dark, they emerge from their dreary shelter.

"It's pitch black tonight," comments Rosalie.

"That's good. No soldiers will be entering the woods on a moonless night. I can risk a small fire," says Pétard, feeling the ground for the stick pile.

"Pépère, will we be staying in the wigwam again tomorrow?" asks Fidèle.

"I'm not sure. At sunrise, I'll go climb the beech tree to make sure the soldiers have left the area. If I don't return, stay here. And you'd better not follow me; it might endanger the others. Stay put!"

"Be careful," utters Rosalie.

"Don't worry. I will be."

Prémélia changes the subject. "Pépère, did Kitpou ever tell you anything more about the bouhine, besides what he told us?"

Before Pétard can answer, Fidèle interjects, "I hope I never see her again!"

Prémélia adds mockingly, "I noticed since you've seen the bouhine, you're uneasy whenever you see a raven or crow. I wonder if she really is a malevolent spirit."

"Lia, if you had seen that phantom and heard her cawing, you would know that she's evil."

"Maybe, Fidèle," says Prémélia. "But it seems to me that she saved you from the Redcoats by scaring them off. I'd like to see this powerful bird woman. Mi'kmaw spirits don't scare me as much as the English soldiers do."

Pétard nods in agreement. "Chère, I know nothing else about her, but I feel the same way as you."

## CHAPTER 7

# The Blue Jay

*The next day, after having kept watch over his hill, Pétard peers* into the wigwam.

"The soldiers have gone and probably won't be back for a while. Still, we must continue to be very careful. Their presence here means that Lawrence hasn't finished hunting Acadians."

The others finally step out into the beautiful brightness of day. Blinded by the sunlight, they shut their eyes immediately. Slowly, they try to open them again, blinking and squinting.

"Cla! Cla! Cla! Three moles," teases the grandfather. "Prémélia, would you like to go beaver hunting and learn from the best hunter in Acadie?"

"Oh yes, Pépère!" she answers with a laugh. "It's so good to be out of the dark wigwam and surrounded by bright autumn colours."

Fidèle pipes up, "Well, I'm going fishing. Rosalie, do you want to come with me?"

Surprisingly, Rosalie giggles as she reminisces. "The last time I went fishing, I was a little girl…if you can imagine me little. Well, young man, it would do me no harm to leave this hiding place for a bit. No harm at all."

Relieved to be out of immediate danger and happy to be alive, they take up the tasks at hand with renewed determination.

Pétard boasts of his hunting skills and exaggerates to amuse his granddaughter and himself as they walk. Prémélia does not believe most of his claims, but she is eager to learn how to hunt beaver.

"It's easier to hunt beaver in winter, but I don't want to wait that long. I've been craving thick beaver stew for the past few days. Its fur makes warm clothing, the teeth make excellent blades, and its excess fat is good for cooking."

"And medicine," adds Prémélia.

After an hour's walk, they come to a pond. Prémélia notices gnawed trees, a sign that a beaver dam may be nearby. Pétard motions for her to stay put while he searches the area.

Waiting for him, Prémélia admires the red and orange maples interspersed with yellow birch that border the pond like bright flames. From the corner of her eye, she glimpses a flash of blue—not a Bluecoat, but a blue jay, fluttering in the blazing foliage. It flies toward her, circles overhead, then flies back across the pond and disappears. Prémélia tries to spot it again. As she scans the area, the girl is startled.

Standing on the other side of the pond is a Mi'kmaw woman with long flowing hair, cloaked in brilliant blue. Could they be feathers? The bouhine! It must be the spirit of the bird woman! Prémélia is both frightened and fascinated by the mysterious being facing her.

Slowly, the Mi'kmaw spirit turns her head and points toward a copse of blood-red trees some distance from the pond. She cannot see the woman's face clearly, but Prémélia senses that the bouhine is directing her to the scarlet trees for a good reason. Still, she does not want to disobey her grandfather, who told her to stay put, and dares not yell out to him lest there be soldiers in the area. Awed by the blue-feathered ghost, she wishes that Pétard could see her also. Growing impatient for her grandfather's return, Prémélia turns her head to look for him. When she gazes once more toward the pond, the spirit is gone. Anxious, she wonders if the bouhine's disappearance coincided with the end of the refoul's course up the rivers.

A short time later, Pétard returns.

"Pépère! I saw the bouhine! She's so beautiful…I think she wants to help us. She pointed to the trees over there. We must go now."

"Shhh…We'll go, but stay a few steps behind me."

As they reach the far side, they walk as quietly as possible toward the red maple trees. Pétard stops when he notices a human form beneath the trees. Could there be soldiers? He signals Prémélia to hide and takes out an arrow. With his arrow set, Pétard pulls back his bowstring and walks slowly toward the body. From the bushes, Prémélia is holding her bow and arrow, ready to shoot. She struggles to control her trembling.

A low moan comes from the body.

The old man freezes for an instant and then exclaims, "Kitpou!"

"Friend?" a weak but familiar voice strains.

Pétard sees that Kitpou's legs are badly wounded. His leggings are torn and covered in dried blood. Pétard bends over him.

"Bluecoats…three days…."

"Save your strength, my friend. We're taking you to our wigwam."

Kitpou closes his eyes. Pétard removes his coat to cover his friend.

"Is he dead?" Prémélia whispers, kneeling beside Kitpou.

"No, just unconscious."

Gently tearing away Kitpou's leggings, Pétard assesses the severity of the wounds.

With his knife, Pétard has a difficult time removing the fragments of lead from Kitpou's swollen legs. Prémélia takes some medicinal oil from her pouch and delicately pours some over the wounds. She helps her grandfather cut some birch saplings to make a rough stretcher.

Kitpou is heavy, especially for the girl. They must stop several times along the way. At one of these stops the wounded man regains consciousness. Kitpou strains to speak, labouring over each word. "Redcoats and others…hunting Mi'kmaq and Acadians. Their scalps worth…much silver to soldiers…."

Kitpou closes his eyes.

"Mon Dieu!" Prémélia cries. "Pépère, this can't be true!"

Kitpou has been sleeping for two days when Rosalie yells, "He's awake and he's hungry!"

The others rush into the wigwam, where Rosalie is already helping Kitpou drink broth.

"Can you speak?" Pétard asks.

Kitpou nods. They gather around him, full of questions about the soldiers who pursued him, their family's imprisonment, and the bouhine who helped him. But Pétard stops them so they won't tire Kitpou, and merely asks, "Do you have any news of the Acadian prisoners of Fort Beauséjour?"

Kitpou nods again. Wearily, he looks at the faces that surround him.

"Put aboard vessels headed south to the Thirteen Colonies."

Prémélia throws herself onto her bed of fir twigs and starts to sob. Rosalie puts her arm on the young girl's shaking shoulders, with no hope of consoling her.

"That's far…eh, Pépère?" asks Fidèle, his voice strained.

"Yes, Fidèle, far, far away," Pétard answers sadly.

The old man goes to comfort his grandson, but Fidèle runs off into forest. Pétard, crippled with sorrow, turns his teary eyes heavenward and pleads, "Mon Dieu, please help us."

Deep despair descends upon the hideout.

## CHAPTER 8

# Prayers, Patience, and Potatoes

*That evening, Fidèle comes back from his solitude to sit with* the others. Their hearts are all broken by the news. Even if Jacques and Marie find their way back to Acadie through hostile colonies and the dangers in the forest, it could take years for them to make it to the Memramkouke Valley on foot. This news means years of great misery for their parents in the Thirteen Colonies, and for them, hiding so close to the soldiers at Fort Beauséjour. Will the Grand Dérangement ever end?

That night, only Kitpou is able to sleep. Just before sunrise, Rosalie and the children finally let go of their troubles and fall asleep, but Pétard, still restless, leaves.

Pacing in front of the wigwam, he seeks a way out of their tragic predicament. It is up to him to find a solution for his devastated family. Little by little, he feels his courage coming back. By the time the sun is strong enough to warm his balding head, he cuts another notch on the time stick, marking the 385th day in hiding. He enters the wigwam with renewed determination.

Pétard bends over Rosalie's bed and whispers in her ear, "Ma belle, I need you to be very courageous."

Half-awake from her troubled sleep, she answers wearily, "Courage? I've none left. None. I might as well give myself up to the British. At least I'll have a roof over my head in prison and in the Thirteen Colonies."

"We're going to survive this Grand Dérangement by staying right here…with the help of prayers, patience, and potatoes."

"Potatoes? Oh, Pétard, you've not slept at all. Potatoes!"

"That's true. But I do mean potatoes. I saved some to plant in the small clearing upstream. I wanted to surprise you again. I need you, Rosalie à Vieux Louis. What would I do with no one to scold me?" he teases affectionately. "Please don't give yourself up to the soldiers. Don't abandon us. For Fidèle and Prémélia's sake, please stay." He squeezes her hand.

Rosalie looks at his sleeping grandchildren, who may be orphans. Her eyes well up. She turns to him and whispers tenderly, "Prayers, patience, potatoes, and you, Pétard. Well, I suppose it won't do me too much harm to live in the forest like a Mi'kmaw woman for a while longer. Cold, damp prisons and the dank, stinking holds of old ships would be even worse for my rheumatism. Cher, I hope to live long enough to see you dance a jig on your hill again."

"You will, ma belle, on our wedding day."

"Mon escrable," she utters tenderly.

Pétard smiles, his eyes beginning to water.

When he kisses her hand, Rosalie sheds a tear.

"Go back to sleep, chère. I'll care for Kitpou until you wake up."

Their resolve is just a small comfort. Nevertheless, they both manage a brave smile.

Rosalie goes back to sleep just as Kitpou awakens. Pétard fetches a goblet of water and helps him drink it. When his friend closes his eyes, Pétard finally sits down. His mind wanders to Jacques and Marie. He prays they are on the same ship as their baby.

After a few hours, Prémélia wakes up and with swollen, red eyes, looks at her grandfather. Pétard goes to her, and they embrace silently.

"We're going to make it through these awful times, ma petite."

Fidèle, who has just woken, overhears his grandfather.

"How can we do that, Pépère?"

"By staying hidden until the end of the war, Fidèle."

"Had I not hidden and stayed with Maman and Papa, I could've killed some soldiers with my arrows so they could escape."

"Fidèle, you know that your father didn't want you to fight. It's an army against unarmed farmers. Without the help of French soldiers, our only defence is to hide."

Frustrated, the young boy pushes the wigwam's deerskin door aside and dashes outside. Why were Acadians so trusting of the British? How were so many tricked? He thinks of his parents, imprisoned in the hold of an English ship. What is going to happen to the deported Acadians once the boats dock in the Thirteen Colonies?

These reflections anger him, and Fidèle suddenly thinks of Beausoleil Broussard, who always refused to trust the English. Since some women and children along the Petcoudiac River were captured, Beausoleil and his men have been harassing the British soldiers.

Fidèle rushes back inside the wigwam and declares, "Pépère, I want to join Beausoleil!"

"Fidèle, he won a few skirmishes, but even Beausoleil and his men can't stop an army. He must always retreat to hide in the woods, like us. Kitpou told me Lawrence has been promoted to governor, and he hasn't forgotten his defeat on the Petcoudiac at the hands of Capitaine Boishébert, his Mi'kmaw and Maliseet allies, and some young Acadians. After what Lawrence has done to innocent families, you can be sure he'll punish the ones who dare to fight back."

Just when Fidèle's enthusiasm is starting to wane, Kitpou, who has been listening from his bed, reveals, "My friend Beausoleil is now planning to bring back the deported Acadians from the Thirteen Colonies by boat."

Hearing this unexpected good news, Fidèle mouth is agape. Finally, there is real hope for finding his parents, whom he misses terribly! Beausoleil always succeeds in his deeds! Fidèle pictures himself alongside Beausoleil, rescuing his parents and sailing home together. His heart aches for this joyful reunion.

"I must go with Beausoleil! I must! Please, Pépère, let me sail with Beausoleil to find Maman and Papa and bring them home!"

"By boat!" shouts Pétard. "With the Baie Française full of enemy ships? That's crazy! We have to wait for the war to end. The English in the Thirteen Colonies greatly outnumber us and the British want to banish us from Acadie. Even if some Acadians come back, Lawrence will just keep deporting them farther and farther away from here."

"Please, Pépère, let me join Beausoleil! It's the only chance we have of finding Maman and Papa. You must let me go and find them!"

Taken aback by his grandson's pleas, Pétard shouts, "No, Fidèle! Our family has been separated once already. I don't want to lose another member!"

For the next few days, Fidèle sulks, barely speaking to anyone.

As the days go by, Prémélia and Pétard seem to undertake their daily chores with more zeal. Even Rosalie is keeping up her courage, as promised. Kitpou recovers from his wounds quickly and, despite difficulty walking, helps to gather provisions for the winter.

One cold and grey afternoon, Kitpou limps through the woods to find Fidèle. The boy, still preferring to hunt alone, is leaning against an old poplar tree, repairing his bow. Kitpou greets him.

Fidèle, still bitter about his grandfather's refusal to let him leave, just grunts.

"I'm leaving your camp tomorrow, Fidèle."

"I wish *I* could leave!"

"You see that wasp's nest up there? It's higher than usual. This means that there will be a lot more snow this winter. Beausoleil will be leaving the Petcoudiac to look for Acadians at the beginning of the Great Snows."

"If only Pépère would let me go!"

"He might give his permission for you to leave if you become a man the Mi'kmaw way. Your grandfather respects the customs of my people. When a Mi'kmaw boy kills his first moose and performs the ritual of the first slain moose, he becomes a man. It'll be easier to hunt down a moose when the snow is deep. If you kill the sacred animal our way, your grandfather will understand that you're no longer a child. He may let you go then. Kill a moose at the very beginning of the Great Snows, and I'll speak of you to Beausoleil."

"You will? Please, tell me about the ceremony!"

"After killing the animal, take out the heart and liver and cook them yourself. You must serve your family first, starting with the eldest down to the youngest."

Fidèle makes a silent promise to remember the knowledge Kitpou has given him. It may be his only chance.

Kitpou leaves after a few weeks, having kept Fidèle's plans a secret. The boy is in better spirits following Kitpou's departure. If Fidèle succeeds, he will join his friend at the la Pointe Rocheuse. Together, they will cross the Petcoudiac River to meet Beausoleil.

# THE RESISTANCE

## CHAPTER 9
# The Moose

*Three months pass before the conditions become favourable for* Fidèle to hunt moose alone. Despite these perfect conditions, he dares to walk farther than Pétard allows.

Fidèle searches all day for signs of the animal. In the dwindling light of late afternoon, a grey jay lands in a nearby conifer. His grandfather calls these jays "moose birds." This one is particularly friendly and rather large...*My sister might be right about the bouhine helping us!* he thinks.

As he approaches the bird, Fidèle spots moose tracks. He follows them and soon locates the large moose struggling through deep snow. Fidèle can barely contain his excitement. The great animal senses the hunter's presence and tries to move faster. Knowing all too well the feeling of being hunted, Fidèle feels pity for the moose. Still, he must not miss his chance to help save his parents. Beausoleil might be leaving within days.

Fidèle stands squarely in place, steadies himself, focuses, and calms his breath. Slowly, without making a sound, he takes an arrow from his quiver, sets it on the string, draws it back, aims carefully, and shoots.

The arrow penetrates the animal's lungs, but the moose keeps up its struggle in the snow for a few minutes before slowing down. The boy dares to approach the animal and sends another arrow through its heart. The moose stops moving and breathes its last breath. Fidèle draws his first breath as a man.

He did it! His first moose! Fidèle silently gives thanks to the venerated moose that has made him a man. But is he really a man? To convince his grandfather, he must believe it himself.

Fidèle cuts into the warm flesh. He removes the heart and liver and places them in his leather bag. He then covers the moose with snow, hoping that no hungry animal will find it. Fidèle will return the next day with his family to clean the carcass of its meat and hide. For the time being, he takes only the organs necessary for the coming-of-age ritual.

On his way back to the wigwam, Fidèle thinks of the preparation he must carry out. He hopes that Pétard will allow him to leave as a man. Fidèle does not want to miss his chance to join Beausoleil and bring back his family from the hostile colonies of the South.

At the wigwam, Fidèle proudly shows the contents of his bag.

"A moose! Cla! Cla! Cla! And you're only twelve years old! Your parents would be so proud of you!"

Pétard gives his grandson a bear hug, and so does Prémélia.

"What a good provider you are," compliments Rosalie. "I'll cook it right away. You were gone for so long. You must be ravenous."

"Thank you, Rosalie, but I want to cook the meal myself," insists Fidèle, looking at Pétard.

His grandfather stops smiling.

"Don't tell me that you're going to serve it yourself, Fidèle."

"Yes, Pépère. In accordance with the Mi'kmaw custom, I'll serve it. If you accept me as a man the Mi'kmaw way, Kitpou will take me to Beausoleil."

At these words, Pétard steps outside the wigwam, followed by Rosalie. Pétard squeezes his head in despair, then stares ahead. Rosalie gently rests her hand on his shoulder before speaking to him softly.

"Pétard, you can't hold him back any longer."

"I won't let another family member be separated from us. The war will end, and no matter who wins, Acadians will return to Acadie. I won't let my little Fidèle go with that reckless Beausoleil! Going into enemy territory in the middle of a war to bring back Acadian families is a great danger to all of them."

"Pétard, now it's my turn to ask for your courage. Let him go, cher. I remember when you were his age. You left your father's home for adventure and no one could stop you. Put yourself in his place. All that boy thinks about is finding his parents. His desire to find them grows stronger by the day. Sooner or later he'll pursue his dangerous quest without your permission. Fidèle is more like you than his father. He'll leave someday soon without telling you, and then you'll regret not giving him your blessing."

Pétard slowly turns around, and Rosalie embraces him.

"You're right, Rosalie. I have to let him go. I pray that my blessing will give my brave little grandson more strength."

Early the next morning, they walk to the moose's body and peel off its hide. Pétard and Fidèle hack the frozen meat with an axe. Prémélia and Rosalie pack the food, which they will feast on for many days after Fidèle's departure.

"We must leave the carcass near the bushes, Fidèle. To appease the animal's spirit, I will bury it at spring thaw," promises Pétard.

Prémélia adds softly, "I want to help you do it, Pépère."

Having finished their last chore together as a family, Pétard and his grandchildren walk quietly, with heavy hearts.

At the wigwam, Rosalie serves them their last meal together: moose meat and spruce tea. Fighting off tears, they eat in silence because it is time for Fidèle to leave. He wishes to avoid sad goodbyes, but everyone's eyes are glistening as they take their turn to embrace him.

"Take good care of yourself, my brother. I will miss you," says Prémélia, choking back tears as they embrace.

Fidèle whispers in her ear, "I had help from the bouhine, but don't tell Pépère until I'm gone, in case he changes his mind about me leaving. You were right. She is watching over us."

They smile at each other and Prémélia hugs him one more time. Wanting to lessen the sadness, she teases, "I'll think of you covered in burrs like a big porcupine when I gather burdock!"

Sniffling, Rosalie tells him, "You'll find your parents because you're a brave young man. I'll pray for your safe return, Fidèle."

Pétard places his hands on his grandson's shoulders.

"Tell Beausoleil I think that he's still a little crazy but very brave, and tell Kitpou we would welcome a visit from him. As for you, Fidèle à Jacques à Pétard, I bless you and your quest to find Jacques and Marie and my new grandchild. Remember, my brave grandson, we won't stop praying for you. Go find them and bring them back safely."

Pétard embraces his grandson one last time. With flowing tears, Prémélia and the old couple watch Fidèle walk away.

At the stream, Fidèle musters his courage and looks back at his devastated family. He declares confidently, "I will bring them back, and we will celebrate together on la Butte-à-Pétard!

Hearing these words, they smile proudly through their tears, hoping that they are not the last words they ever hear from Fidèle.

After a long trek in snowshoes, Fidèle reaches the hill near the Pierre à Michel farms, from where he can see the dyke bordering the brown Petcoudiac River. Walking along the edge of the forest, he notices two chimneys towering over snow-covered rubble, where once stood the homes of the Vincent brothers. *Did those families have enough time to get away?* he wonders.

He forges on to the Mi'kmaw camp near la Pointe Rocheuse. He comes upon the eerie sight of ten Mi'kmaw funeral platforms, high up in the trees, out of reach of animals until their spring burial. His grandfather has told him that the dead are wrapped in fur with their knees bent against their chest. Could these people have been killed by soldiers?

Finally, he arrives at the deserted Mi'kmaw camp. There is only one wigwam left. Fidèle steps on a branch, making it crack. The noise alerts a Mi'kmaw man, who pulls aside the wigwam's deerskin flap and pokes his head outside. His face, painted completely black, startles Fidèle, who greets him in the Mi'kmaw language.

"You're now a man," the man with the painted face replies.

"Kitpou! It's you! Yes, I killed my first moose and performed the ritual just as you told me to! Pépère actually gave me his blessing! Oh…and he said that he'd like you to visit him."

"Enter," orders Kitpou, his voice sounding weak.

In the wigwam, Kitpou lies down and closes his eyes. *It's not like Kitpou to take a nap when someone is about to share news. Is he not well?* Fidèle expected more of a response from him. Out of respect, he dares not say a word. Judging by his blackened face, Kitpou is in mourning. Something is wrong. He seems much thinner and there are spots under the facepaint. After a few moments, as if he has been gathering strength, Kitpou speaks in a strained voice.

"Beausoleil has a vessel anchored upriver from Le Coude. He plans to come this way tomorrow to harass the enemy once more. He's not quite ready to go to the Thirteen Colonies, but he welcomes you to join him at his camp. I have smallpox, but I still have enough strength to take you across the river."

Fidèle wants to know more about Beausoleil, but he realizes that Kitpou could be gravely ill and needs help.

"Where are the other Mi'kmaq?"

"Those who didn't die of smallpox went north."

"Did the ones on the platforms all die of smallpox?" Fidèle knows the smallpox is serious, and that the disease has ravaged the Mi'kmaq since the coming of the White Man.

"Yes," Kitpou says solemnly.

"I'll stay until you get better!"

"No. It's too late for me to get well. But I want to take you to Beausoleil. Then I'll join my people at the winter camp. That is where I want to die. Now, I must sleep."

Fidèle's heart is so heavy with sorrow that he must step out of the wigwam. Outside, he puts on his snowshoes and walks to the bank of the Petcoudiac. He looks upriver toward Le Coude, not far from where Beausoleil's boat is anchored, but it is too far away to see. He tries not to think about his worried family at the hideout and Kitpou's grave illness. His mind wanders. Should he stay to help Kitpou? Should he go back to protect his sister, his grandfather, and Rosalie? It takes all of Fidèle's willpower to concentrate on his mission: join Beausoleil and bring back the rest of his family to Acadie.

## CHAPTER 10

# The Seagulls

*Fidèle wakes very early the next morning, too anxious to go* back to sleep. He goes outside and sits on a log. He had taken a risk sleeping in a wigwam with Kitpou; he knows that smallpox easily moves from one person to another, but it was a choice between that and freezing outside. Before him is an opening in the pine branches that frames, like a painting, the view from the rocky point. Above the brown Chipoudie Bay, he sees the dark line of the faraway coast of the Baie Française, and above it the grey sky.

Kitpou soon joins him. Fidèle keeps staring ahead, waiting for him to speak. After a few minutes, he notices a speck on the horizon.

"Kitpou…look, a ship!" says Fidèle.

"The English. There may be more on their way. This one is heading to Fort Beauséjour. There'll be a thick fog today. It'll conceal us from the enemy."

At noon, Kitpou and Fidèle leave. It is low tide, when British ships are least likely to sail upstream. Fidèle is grateful that Kitpou still has the strength and the will to help him. With the canoe hoisted on their shoulders, they slowly struggle around patches of ice and boulder-sized chunks of frozen mud on the shore. They could easily slip and damage the canoe or even drown in the freezing current. Fidèle is relieved when they eventually make it to the river.

Crossing Chipoudie Bay in the thick winter fog, Fidèle worries they are not going in the right direction. Maybe Kitpou's sickness is affecting his sense of direction. Fidèle thinks they may be lost, but he dares not say it. He is surprised when they finally reach Cap des Demoiselles. Because the tide is higher now, most of the huge chunks of frozen mud have been carried away by the strong current. Fidèle sets foot ashore.

"Beausoleil will be on the lookout for Pétard's grandson waiting here at the beginning of the Great Snows. I pray that you'll find your parents, Fidèle," says Kitpou.

"Thank you for helping all of us. We won't forget your great kindness. Please, Kitpou, go and see my sister. She has herbs that may help you," pleads Fidèle, fighting back tears.

Without answering, Kitpou looks knowingly into the young man's eyes and shakes his hand.

"Adieu, Kitpou. I'll pray for you, too," Fidèle says. With tears in his eyes, he pushes the canoe back into the bay. Kitpou turns the canoe and waves before crossing the bay. Fidèle knows that he will never see him again.

Once Kitpou has completely disappeared from sight, Fidèle searches the riverside for a hiding place, just in case an English ship crosses the bay.

He finds a thicket of short spruce trees where he can hide and still catch sight of Beausoleil's vessel. In the middle of the trees, he cuts a few branches to make a bed on the snow. Exhausted, he lies down inside the palisade of evergreens.

Overwhelmed by the emotions of the last few days, Fidèle weeps for Kitpou and his own family. *Will there be no Mi'kmaq or Acadians left after the British finish hunting them down? Am I really man enough to find my parents and bring them back?* For a moment, he wants to abandon his quest and run back to his grandfather. Then he thinks of his poor parents, who must need him the most.

He waits and waits. Maybe he will have to make camp for a few days before Beausoleil Broussard shows up. His mind wanders. *I must be near the Bruns' house. I should be able to see their thatched roof from here. It must have been torched by the soldiers. Their neighbours' homes must have burned. The Légers, Breaus, Comeaus….*

A piercing cry makes him jump. Was it a person or an animal? Where did it come from? Cautiously, Fidèle rises and crouches behind his little fortress of trees to scan the surroundings.

The heavy fog gradually dissipates. In the water nearest the shore, he makes out the large rock formations of Cap des Demoiselles. Seagulls land on the snow-capped rocks, awaiting the refoul and the fish that the big wave stirs up. Was it a gull's cry that startled him? The tide will soon be coming in.

Suddenly, there is the dark outline of a vessel in the middle of the misty bay! Beausoleil? As if answering his question, a fog patch lifts for a few seconds, showing the vessel clearly. It seems to be coming from Fort Beauséjour. A British ship!

Frightened, Fidèle drops to his knees to hide. He watches through the branches as it approaches. The silent monster sails toward the Cap des Demoiselles, on its way up the Petcoudiac River.

*The English sailors didn't see me,* thinks Fidèle. *They must be going to attack Beausoleil! If he and his men have set sail, they have no chance of escaping!*

The fog continues to lift, revealing a stunning sight. The seagulls on the rocks take on the forms of Mi'kmaw women cloaked in white. On the biggest rock, the largest of the gulls transforms into the bouhine, her cape of shocking white feathers contrasted against the dark grey sky. Fidèle is awestruck. The bouhine and the women slowly raise their arms to the sky as the refoul swells up higher and higher. This wave, now gigantic, crashes into the enemy ship with such force that two sailors are thrown overboard. The shaken crew struggles to rescue them. The fog descends again like a curtain. Over the muffled cries of the crew, Fidèle hears the captain yell orders in English. Finally, the

The Seagulls ⚓ 69

shouting dies out as the fog begins to clear once more. The British vessel is gone, as are the spirits. At high tide, the big rocks look like tiny islands. Fidèle waits, shrouded by the fog.

All of a sudden, a ship's bow cuts through the mist. The British sailors have spotted him! Fidèle starts running away from the shore.

"Ohé! Could that be a little Pétard running from Redcoats? Come back! The English have left for now, and the fog will keep us safe!"

Fidèle stops and turns around. Overjoyed, he runs toward the shore.

"Beausoleil!"

Captain Beausoleil sings out, "Partons, la mer est belle, Fidèle! Ha! Ha! Haaa!"

That night, Prémélia and Pétard dream that Fidèle is saved by a large, luminous seagull.

## CHAPTER 11
# The Root Cellar

*A few days after Fidèle's departure, the old couple are alone at* the hideout. Rosalie sees an eagle land near the wigwam.

"Saint Esprit! It's as if that eagle wants your attention!"

Pétard, repairing a snowshoe, looks up and stops his work. Both eagle and man stare at each other.

"I think I know what this strange behaviour means. The Mi'kmaq would say that the person bearing the bird's name has died. I fear that we'll never see our friend Kitpou again. God bless him."

As if to confirm Pétard's belief, the eagle flies away.

"Kitpou was a very good man. I wonder if my little Fidèle was with him when he died."

Rosalie sets her kindling down to comfort Pétard.

After the period of the Great Snows, the weather becomes unseasonably warm, which spoils most of their meat reserves. After a few days, the deep snow melts away. But winter takes hold again, this time with extreme cold. Without the thick blanket of snow insulating the wigwam, they must cover it with more evergreen boughs. The bitter winds make hunting very difficult, and food becomes so scarce that soon they are close to starving. It also brings illness to Rosalie and Pétard, who are too sick to do anything but keep the fire going.

Weak with hunger, Prémélia leaves them for another attempt at hunting.

"If la petite doesn't kill an animal today, we'll have to eat poplar bark and mashcoui again. Otherwise, we'll starve to death," sighs Rosalie.

"Kitpou told me that we could also eat boiled moccasins and rabbit droppings to avoid starvation."

"Stop your nonsense."

"Cla! Cla! No, it's true. That's what the Mi'kmaq do to survive when there is no food."

Strenuously, Pétard gets up and places another log on the small fire they have maintained night and day since the beginning of the cold snap. He then cuts another notch in one of the wigwam's centre poles.

"It has now been 560 days in hiding! We are tough old birds, you and me."

Prémélia bursts into the wigwam, holding her trophy—a dead skunk.

"Meat!" she announces triumphantly.

"Saint Esprit!"

"Skunk meat isn't bad," says Pétard. "Prémélia, I'll show you how to clean it. I learned of a trick to take away the smell."

"Rosalie, the fat would be good to rub on your joints to soothe your rheumatism," says the girl.

"The fat may ease your pain," adds Pétard, "but you won't smell like a rose!"

"Never will I cover myself in stinky skunk grease. Never! But I'll eat the meat. It should taste better than boiled hide and animal droppings.

"Cla! Cla! Cla!"

"Don't laugh, Pépère. Kitpou once told me that the fat can also make hair grow," teases Prémélia.

"And you sure need some on your hard old noggin. You'll have to spare us from the stench, though. Maybe cover it with a fur hat," says Rosalie.

"Do you think that I'd be more handsome in a skunk-fur hat, ma belle?"

"You old fool!" snaps Rosalie.

They all share a rare laugh.

Prémélia wastes no time in skinning the skunk and cooking the meat. Seeing them eating and bantering gives hope to Prémélia that they will get well.

The next morning, Prémélia stokes the fire to make some spruce tea. After serving them a goblet of the warm brew and leftover skunk meat, she puts her hand on their foreheads.

"Your fevers are going down."

"You see, my Rose? Skunk meat is a good cure."

"I hope I have more luck hunting today," says Prémélia. The young girl dons her peaked Mi'kmaw hat and tunic made from her brother's sacred moose.

"I'm going with you, ma petite."

"Oh no, Pépère! Please wait until you're well enough."

"Listen to her, Pétard. She's right."

"All right, I'll listen. Be very prudent, chère."

"Don't worry, Pépère. I'm always careful."

After Prémélia leaves, Rosalie asks, "Why did you caution her so, today?"

"When I woke up this morning, the first thought that entered my mind was that danger is very near."

"Mon cher Pétard, we've been living near danger for over a year. Prémélia has been the most prudent of all."

The forest is silent, as if the great cold has frozen nature's sounds. Prémélia sets rabbit snares made of spruce roots on their well-trodden paths. Then she looks for vapour coming from holes in the ground, as well as droppings and broken twigs; all signs of an animal's presence.

At the forest's edge, she finally sees a muskrat making its way toward la Butte-à-Pétard. Her fear of starving clouds her judgment. Despite the danger of walking across a field, Prémélia pursues the animal straight out into the open. Midway between la Butte and the woods, she shoots one arrow into the muskrat. The animal stops moving. Prémélia is relieved to provide food for a few more days. She runs over to her prey, pulls out the arrow, and grabs the dead animal by the tail. It must have been starving too; it does not weigh very much.

When she looks up, she realizes that she is closer to her old home than she thought. Instead of returning to the security of the forest, she is drawn closer by the happy memories that come flooding back.

Once atop la Butte, she sees that all that is left in the charred rubble are the fireplace and the root cellar. Overwhelmed with nostalgia, she walks to the cellar, which seems intact. Maybe there are some old jars they could use. The trapdoor is frozen shut. She lays the muskrat on the ground and tries to open the door with both hands, to no avail. She picks up a stone and hits the door several times before it loosens.

Suddenly, she notices a red blur out of the corner of her eye. Looking up, she sees a patrol of Redcoats moving across the marsh toward la Butte. Terrified, she pulls the door open with all her might, almost forgetting to grab the muskrat. Awkward with fear, she stumbles and falls into the cellar.

Prémélia hits the earthen floor face down. She is so scared that she doesn't even feel the pain of her landing. In the darkness, she struggles to control her terror by telling herself that the soldiers are too far away to have seen her. Fortunately, because of the frozen earth and lack of snow, she has left no footprints. *Why would soldiers stop to poke around rubble in this severe cold?* Trembling, she sits up and prays silently.

A shout in English makes her heart jump. Prémélia holds her breath and waits. Hearing nothing, she breathes, but dares not move. *Was that an order to march in a different direction?* Prémélia does not realize that a soldier has been sent to search la Butte as the others walk on to the next hamlet. First, he checks the ruins of a neighbour's farm, and then he proceeds toward Prémélia's old home. *Where are they going? Maybe toward the hideout? Oh nooo! Will Pépère and Rosalie hear them coming in time to hide in a wigwam? What's that noise coming from the Hébert home? An animal poking around? A soldier? Oh mon Dieu, mon Dieu!*

Her heart is beating so loudly that she doesn't hear the footsteps until they near the cellar door. *Moccasins don't make a noise. It's the sound of a soldier's boots!* He stops. Prémélia holds her breath. The trapdoor opens, and the sudden brightness of day blinds her for a few seconds. The tall soldier looms in the doorway, right before her, his face shadowed by his hat. Petrified, she cannot even scream. To her surprise, the Redcoat whispers softly, "Do not fret," and then closes the trapdoor.

Prémélia does not understand the soldier's English words, but she realizes that the gentleness in his voice meant that he was sparing her. Or was it a trick? She waits for a while before opening the door a crack. The kind soldier has already joined the others, who continue upriver.

Once the Redcoats are no longer in sight, she bolts from the root cellar. She promises herself never to return to la Butte-à-Pétard until the end of the war.

## CHAPTER 12

# The Guest

*At last, the great cold ends and snow falls in abundance, covering* the wigwam and protecting its occupants from the cold. The snow also makes hunting larger animals easier for Prémélia in her snowshoes. Despite this change, Prémélia is worried. *Dear God, please don't take away the rest of my family.*

Pétard and Rosalie recover slowly. At first they are only able to help each other get up and sip broth. Because their legs are so weak, they must hold on to each other to move about in the wigwam. Day by day, they manage small chores as they regain their strength, their appetite, and the will to live, if only for the sake of their dear Prémélia. When they finally feel strong again, they joyfully gather firewood to surprise their little hunter, relieved to no longer be a burden.

One fine morning, Prémélia climbs the lookout tree as usual to check for soldiers at la Butte. All she sees is the mournful sight of a few chimneys standing like gravestones.

Despite her sadness, she is thankful for being alive. Every day, the same questions gnaw at her heart. How can she know if the war is over when they must stay in hiding? Is Fidèle in trouble? Will her family come back? Her old neighbours? The Mi'kmaq? What if no one comes back?

The faint flutter of little wings and happy chirping herald the arrival of the black-capped chickadees that perch delicately around Prémélia. Her tame little friends make her smile. She takes a few seeds from her pocket and holds out her hand, inviting the tiny birds to come and eat. One is rounder and fluffier than the rest. *Could this ball of feathers be the bouhine, come to help me?*

Prémélia does not notice the Mi'kmaw man climbing up the bank of the river.

Once her tiny guests are satisfied, she looks up toward la Butte. That is when Prémélia spots the man who is already making camp at the abandoned Mi'kmaw site. She wonders who, except for Kitpou, would dare canoe up the Memramkouke in the middle of winter. Maybe the man has news. Should she go and spy on him?

Prémélia climbs down from the tree as fast as she can and follows the muddy stream. She stays in the shadows of the evergreens and takes care not to step on dead branches. When she finally has a better view of the campsite, the man is gone. Where did he go? She advances slowly. A sudden noise makes her stop to listen. She makes out the sound of snowshoes coming her way. He must have seen her!

Even though the Mi'kmaq are friends of the Acadians, Prémélia knows that a young girl must be wary of strangers. Rushing to her hideout now would endanger her elders, but this man is moving too fast. She can't hide. Prémélia just has time to point her bow and arrow toward the sound of snowshoes coming from behind the clump of fir trees.

The stranger stops in his tracks when he sees the little hunter ready to shoot him. Motionless, they both stare at each other. Prémélia recognizes the young man's piercing blue eyes.

"Jean-Charles à Violette!" she exclaims.

"Prémélia à Jacques à Pétard?"

The two young people embrace. Before the Grand Dérangement, Jean-Charles regularly visited the Mi'kmaw camp at the foot of la Butte, but Prémélia did not know him well. He was older, and she had always felt a little intimidated by him.

"The last time that I saw you, I was returning from fishing poulamon," reminisces Jean-Charles. "You were with your grandfather and your little brother. Fidèle had slipped and fallen into the river. He was covered in mud from head to toe!"

Remembering the pouting boy and his grinning grandfather, they share a good laugh.

Prémélia invites Jean-Charles to the hideout. On the way, she tells him about their escape from la Butte up to the time of Fidèle's departure.

"I was his age when I left to search for my Mi'kmaw father. But your little brother is on a far more dangerous quest. And you chose danger as well, hiding so close to enemy forts." The attractive young man smiles and adds, "Never would I have believed that the little Pétard girl would become a hunter."

Just then, her grandfather bounds from the bushes.

"What a *tintamarre*! Rosalie thinks that you're Redcoats coming to hunt us down. Jean-Charles! It's so good to see you!" Pétard welcomes him with open arms.

To their disappointment, Jean-Charles does not have any news of their family or neighbours, but he tells them that soldiers are still hunting escaped Acadian and Mi'kmaw people, under Lawrence's orders. Despite the bad news, Jean-Charles's visit is very much appreciated…especially by Prémélia.

For three very enjoyable days, Jean-Charles helps them with their chores, devours Rosalie's delicious fricots, and converses mostly with Pétard…while discreetly observing Prémélia.

Prémélia notices that Rosalie is unusually quiet, and she isn't laughing or smiling at his stories the way the other two are. *Rosalie barely speaks to Jean-Charles. It's as if she dislikes him!*

Soon it is time for Jean-Charles to leave.

"Come with me to Louisbourg," he says to them all. "Île Royale is still French, and the fortress would be safer than staying here."

"Don't worry about us," answers Pétard. "We're better off here. The French soldiers at Louisbourg want young men like you, who are ready to fight. The English won't be satisfied until they capture Louisbourg again. They are determined to rid the land of every single Frenchman and Acadian. Take good care of yourself, young man."

The two men hug. Rosalie lets herself be embraced, showing no emotion. When it is Prémélia's turn, Jean-Charles holds her longer. He looks at her one last time. Prémélia manages to hold back tears and bids him farewell with a little tremor in her voice.

After he leaves, Prémélia says to her grandfather, "Let's go check our snares."

That is the code that Prémélia and Pétard use when they want to speak privately.

When they are out of Rosalie's earshot, Prémélia asks, "Why is Rosalie so unfriendly to Jean-Charles?"

"She thinks his father was one of the Mi'kmaw men who burned Beaubassin, but she can't be certain because the men she saw had painted faces."

"But Pépère, it was the French who ordered the Mi'kmaq to burn their homes. They didn't want the English soldiers to use the houses for cover!"

"Rosalie knows the Mi'kmaq and French have always been allies and they had to follow the French officers' orders. But Rosalie wants to blame the Mi'kmaq. My Rose has a few thorns, eh?"

Pétard rests his arm on his granddaughter's shoulders and says tenderly, "Jean-Charles is a valiant young man. I see that you like him a lot. Am I right?"

Prémélia nods. "I hope he comes to visit again."

"So do I, chère."

En route to Île Royale, Jean-Charles finds himself growing more and more conflicted about leaving the trio to survive on their own. And he remembers the little tremor in Prémélia's voice. Could she be feeling the same way as him? Jean-Charles admits to himself that he has fallen in love. It's like nothing he has ever felt before.

Suddenly he stops in his tracks. What is he doing? The company of brave Prémélia is more important than the company of French soldiers. He makes a decision and turns abruptly in his tracks, retracing his steps to the hideout, feeling more and more elated about his good choice. There, he finds Rosalie, who eyes him with suspicion.

"I can't leave the three of you without strong defences," he affirms confidently.

"Don't change your plans just to court Prémélia. She's only fourteen years old."

"My mother was her age when she married my father," he answers, taken aback.

Hearing this, Rosalie can no longer hold back the suppressed anger that has been burning inside her.

"Exactly! Your mother was too young to know better than to marry a Mi'kmaw! No wonder she returned to her parents when you were still an infant on her back. And when you were a boy, you broke your mother's heart by leaving her to search for your father. That's what killed her!"

Jean-Charles is stunned by the cruel words and, despite being nineteen years old, struggles not to cry. He defends himself in a trembling voice. "Maman died because of poor health. She wanted me to find my father."

"You can't have Prémélia! Never! Go away!"

Stung, Jean-Charles leaves abruptly.

Rosalie, shocked by her own cruelty, lies down and whimpers in shame. What has she just done? If Prémélia and Pétard find out that she banished Jean-Charles, they will never forgive her. She bites down on her lips as if to seal in her awful secret.

SPRING 1763

# THE REUNION

## CHAPTER 13

# The End of the War

*On her eighth spring in the woods, Prémélia is twenty years* old. From the big branch of the beech tree, she admires the radiant valley carpeted with bright green grass and the first dandelions of the season. With the gleam of the morning sun, the winding, red-brown river now resembles a silver ribbon. The puddles in the marsh are like pieces of a shattered mirror under the brilliant blue sky. After the past winter, the harshest of all, this beautiful sight brings her some solace. Cold and famine have nearly killed Pétard and Rosalie, who have aged considerably as a result. Rosalie still has no appetite and suffers great pain in her bones. The old woman has lost a lot of her will to live, no matter how much Pétard tries to lift her spirits. Even Pétard is losing hope of ever again living on la Butte. Prémélia does not believe they will be able to endure another winter. Loneliness and worry cloud her thoughts, even on this sunny morning.

She walks back to the hideout and finds Pétard sitting at his favourite spot on a fallen maple. In the small forest clearing, he contemplates the soil of his little potato garden. Since the day he was able to save a few leftover shrivelled potatoes from their old farm, he has proudly planted potatoes every year and maintained this miraculous hidden garden patch.

Pétard does not see his granddaughter arrive. He begins to weep. Knowing her brave grandfather would not want her to see him crying, Prémélia quietly backs away from the clearing. While waiting behind a thicket of evergreens for him to stop weeping, she happens to kneel over a clear pool of water and sees her reflection. It is not like a real mirror. She makes out her tanned face, barely remembering the rosy round face of her childhood. Prémélia grew out of her *capine* years ago, and has been going bare-headed, with her hair loose like the Mi'kmaq. *Will Maman, Papa, and Fidèle recognize me?*

"There's no need to ruin your eyes to see what you look like. You're very good-looking in your Mi'kmaw clothing. You take after my side of the family."

Startled, Prémélia turns and smiles at her grandfather, who has never stopped teasing her through even the worst of times. She guesses that her grandfather saw her backing away out of respect for his privacy.

"Pépère, it's so lovely at la Butte today. Please come with me to take a look."

"My legs are very sore today…it's too long a walk

for old people like Rosalie and me. I don't think we're going to last much longer on this earth."

"Don't say that, Pépère. You always look forward to going upstream to pick fiddleheads, downstream to pick passe-pierre, and to your hill for apples. Besides, you can't miss harvesting the best potatoes in the world!"

"Prémélia, you're a strong young woman. You'll survive."

"Oh, Pépère, you—"

"Shhh! Get down," whispers Pétard, fear in his eyes.

Prémélia huddles with her grandfather.

"What did you hear? Soldiers?" she whispers.

"Look at the bush over there. A man…."

"Could he be an English colonist?"

"No. His clothes are too ragged…. An Acadian?"

At that moment, Pétard recognizes the man and shouts with glee, "Ti-Pruce! You made it back!"

The man jumps at the sudden sound. "Can that be Pétard himself? Don't tell me you stayed here all these years! You stubborn old braggart!"

"I might be old, but I'm still better looking than you!" jokes Pétard as the two friends embrace.

After a few tears of joy, Ti-Pruce turns toward Prémélia and kisses her hand.

"You've grown into a beautiful woman. Thank God, you don't look a bit like your grandfather."

They laugh. Prémélia disregards proper etiquette and hugs Ti-Pruce.

"Ti-Pruce, my old friend," says Pétard, "from where have you sprung?"

"I've been hiding in the woods with a few others all over Acadie. Last week, a couple of English soldiers came across our hideout. I thought they were going to shoot us."

Ti-Pruce pauses and emotion contorts his face.

"They told us that they need Acadians to repair the broken levées because…they had won the war."

"It's over, Pépère. It's over!" cries Prémélia.

Pétard and his grandchild hold on to each other, both weeping.

Respectfully, Ti-Pruce waits until they are ready to listen before continuing.

"It was high time the hunt for Acadians ended. Had I known you were hiding here all that time, my old friend, with little Prémélia…."

"Little! She's not very tall, but this young woman is a skilled hunter! She has kept us all alive since Fidèle left in 1757 to join Beausoleil in his search for his parents and new sibling. They were among the first to be deported. We pray for—"

"What a tintamarre!" shouts Rosalie from the wigwam, her voice very strained. "How can a person sleep in peace around here?"

"Who's that?" asks Ti-Pruce.

Pétard and his granddaughter just grin and take the path to the hideout. Ti-Pruce follows them to the wigwam surrounded by thick evergreens.

"You're clever ones. It is a real Mi'kmaw dwelling, very well hidden."

Ti-Pruce pulls the deerskin curtain to one side, pokes his head in, and sees Rosalie in her bed.

"No, it can't be! Rosalie à Vieux Louis!"

"Saint Esprit! Ti-Pruce! I never thought I would be so glad to see your devilish face."

The three of them join the old woman. Pétard helps her up and gently tells her, "Chère, the war is over."

Rosalie begins to sob.

Pétard, his face streaming with tears, embraces her, saying, "You kept your promise, and we made it through the long war and great hardship. There, there, ma chère Rosalie." The others cannot stop their own flow of emotions, the ones they had stored away deep in their hearts for so long.

Finally, Rosalie stops crying and then blurts out, "We have to stop bawling. There's so much work to do. We must move our camp to la Butte right away! Yes, yes. Right away!"

"That's my Rose. And it's on my hill that we'll finally get married. Ti-Pruce, is there a priest in the vicinity?"

Ti-Pruce laughs and replies, "Not to my knowledge. But if you're in a great rush, I can marry you two…. Next to you, Pétard, I'm the oldest man in the Memramkouke Valley, so I have the authority of a priest."

Pétard takes Rosalie's hand and asks her, "Will you accept your new life on la Butte as my wife?"

"Oh, I suppose, you old fool. What harm can it do, after all we've been through?"

"Cla! Cla! This morning, I thought I had reached the end of my days, but now I'm engaged to be married. I feel like a new man! Yes, we must leave right now, my Rose."

A few days later, on la Butte-à-Pétard, the very brief wedding ceremony is followed by a feast of porcupine and fiddlehead stew. It is a joyous occasion, yet many tears are shed.

That night in the wigwam, where once stood her beloved home, Prémélia thanks her guardian angel. She entered the woods as a twelve-year-old girl and left the woods as a twenty-year-old woman. And just as she has done throughout her adolescence, Prémélia continues to pray for the safe return of her whole family.

## CHAPTER 14
# The Courtship

*The Pétards do not see him coming until he is on their hill.*
Except for his moccasins, the man is groomed like a
gentleman. Sitting in front of their wigwam, they stop
eating their breakfast, wary of the newcomer—for he
is surely not an Acadian. Is he an English landowner?
Will they be asked to leave la Butte?

As the man walks over, they stand up. He stops in
front of them and takes off his elegant three-cornered
hat.

"You've finally returned to your hill," says a familiar voice.

"Not Jean-Charles à Violette!" exclaims Pétard.
"Your Acadian side took over your Mi'kmaw side. But
what are you doing, dressed like a rich gentleman, eh?
That doesn't seem like you."

Jean-Charles laughs and hugs Pétard. Then he
gazes at Prémélia and slowly approaches to embrace her

lovingly. Speechless, the young woman cannot believe that she is in the arms of the man whom she had given up waiting for. He is even more handsome than she remembered.

Jean-Charles loosens his embrace.

"Prémélia, you're as beautiful as ever."

Overwhelmed and embarrassed by his compliment, she puts a rough hand on her tanned face to hide a scratch. Under Jean-Charles's gaze, Prémélia feels her legs weakening, as if she is going to faint.

Surprising everybody, Rosalie walks over to Jean-Charles and hugs him. They all sit down to listen his news.

"I've come from Halifax, where I met with Beausoleil and his brother. They had a ship and were preparing to take Acadian families to settle in the French colony of San Domingue. The British were very glad to see the Beausoleil clan leave the colony. Beausoleil told me that the last time he saw Fidèle was six years ago." Jean-Charles looks at Pétard and says teasingly, "He said your grandson was more impatient than you."

The three smile sadly, dreading the rest of the news.

"Fidèle figured that Beausoleil could not rescue Acadians quickly enough, because he was too busy fighting English soldiers. Fidèle believed that the quickest way to find his parents would be to get himself deported. Beausoleil couldn't dissuade him. So, after having learned some English phrases from a Port-Royal refugee, he left Beausoleil's hideout to give himself up to a patrol of Bluecoats at Le Coude. No one has heard of him since."

Prémélia gasps.

Pétard groans. "I don't want to fathom the hardships my little grandson must have endured in the hostile colonies."

"Letting himself be deported! Saint Esprit!"

"I often dream of my brother. I believe Fidèle's alive," Prémélia quietly reveals.

"So do I, chère," adds Pétard.

Jean-Charles decides to rest at the abandoned Mi'kmaw campsite for a few days. The old couple guess why he really wants to linger at the foot of la Butte. Pétard asks for his help in building their house, knowing that Jean-Charles will readily accept this opportunity to stay longer.

That very day Pétard and Jean-Charles cut down spruce trees and square the logs with their axes. The women make sturdy brooms to sweep away debris and ash from the old earthen floor while the men hew the logs until sundown.

Luckily, the days remain sunny as they build on the foundation stones of the old family home, whose chimney stack is still standing. Ti-Pruce comes by to help them make the thatched roof just in time, before the rain. Having no glass for the windows yet, they hang animal skins like curtains.

Their roof withstands the pouring rain. In the dry and warm one-room home, the women lay fresh spruce boughs along with fragrant balsam fir branches for beds, as they once did in the wigwam. Pétard and Jean-Charles make a rough table and benches, their only furniture.

Since leaving their forest refuge, Rosalie and Prémélia have scrounged the village ruins and found an assortment of jars, pewter goblets, plates, and cutlery, which they saved for their first meal at the table. Prémélia places a cracked blue-and-white vase filled with dandelions at the centre of the table.

"I found it in the ashes of the Hébert home," says Prémélia.

"Remember how often your grandfather and old Hébert argued about who had the best garden?"

Pétard overhears Rosalie.

"Old Hébert and I were not best friends, but I think he and his family would be pleased that we saved their vase."

"I hope the Héberts make it back, Pépére, so we can give it back to them."

"So do I, ma chère. And I wish that someday soon, the rest of our family will join us in our new home."

It feels very strange to be sitting at a table for the first time in twelve years. They are overcome with gratitude and sadness all at once. Teary-eyed, they wait for Jean-Charles.

When Jean-Charles returns from his wigwam, Rosalie fills the bowls with a hearty fricot.

"Your rabbit stew is missing something," says Jean-Charles, sniffing his bowl.

All are dismayed by his comment, for Rosalie is known for her delicious fricot. Before she can retort, Jean-Charles pulls out a bottle from his coat.

"This French wine is what's missing."

They all laugh.

"Now I can say grace," says Pétard, winking.

After the first supper in the new home, Pétard and Jean-Charles go for a walk on the old path in the marsh.

"Pétard, as you know, the English need the Acadians' skills for rebuilding the aboiteaux and the levées. The marshes now belong to the English. You'll have to work for them for a few years, and you might even be forced to leave again if they decide they have no more use for your services."

"My family may have to eventually live elsewhere in Acadie, but we must stay here as long as we can to wait for Fidèle, Jacques, Marie, and the child."

"Pétard, most of the Acadian families that escaped capture had to surrender to avoid starvation after years of hiding in the woods. I admire your endurance, as I do Rosalie's. In regards to Prémélia…." He pauses to gather his courage. "I've loved her with all my heart since our meeting at the hideout. May I have your permission to ask your courageous granddaughter for her hand in marriage?"

"Well, of course! It's high time you asked! For the last few weeks, whenever you look at each other, each of you have had your 'eyes in the butter.' You know… the shiny eyes of love," teases Pétard.

Jean-Charles laughs heartily with the old man and gives him a big hug. But soon he stops, and seems a little serious. "Before I ask Prémélia, I must see Rosalie alone. Please send her to my wigwam, and don't tell the women about my wish to marry Prémélia."

Rosalie's anxiety grows as she walks down the hill and enters the wigwam. With a humble voice, the old woman speaks first.

"You have the right to be angry with me. What I said to you years ago were the words of a distressed and hurt woman. I was still upset over your father setting fire to my house. But he was a warrior following the orders of French officers who thought this would be best for the Acadians of Beaubassin. At the time, I trusted the English and thought it wouldn't make a difference if our village continued to be under British authority. I was wrong. Now I'm glad that those devils aren't warming their boots at the old hearth in my pretty little house. War makes us all crazy, but that's a poor excuse for the harm I've caused. I didn't have the courage to tell Pétard and Prémélia about your wish to stay with us, and about the dishonourable way that I treated you. Please forgive me!"

Jean-Charles smiles kindly at her. "I'll forgive you if you grant me one favour." From a large bag, he gently unrolls an elegant gown of golden silk, trimmed with white lace.

Rosalie gasps. "I've never seen such a beautiful dress! It shines like real gold! Did it belong to royalty?"

"No. A wealthy lady from Louisbourg gave it to me as a reward for helping her escape the fortress before the English siege."

"That's a strange reward for a man. Forgive me, I did not mean—"

"It's strange indeed," agrees Jean-Charles, still smiling, "but the good lady knew of my plans and encouraged me to pursue them. Rosalie, the favour I ask of you is to tailor this dress to Prémélia's size for our wedding."

"Wedding! Oh! That makes me so happy! Yes, yes! I'll fix it for ma chère Prémélia," blurts Rosalie, starting to cry.

When Prémélia notices Jean-Charles and Rosalie walking up the hill, her heart skips a beat, hoping that her wish might come true. Jean-Charles goes straight to her and looks into her lovely green eyes.

"For years, I fought the Redcoats and Bluecoats. I witnessed the burning of Acadie. I saw so many Acadian and Mi'kmaw families decimated by separation, starvation, smallpox, and death. Through it all, it was the memory of you keeping watch in your tree, patiently waiting to return to your village, that gave me the will to continue. I love you, Prémélia. Will you be my wife?"

Prémélia answers by throwing herself in his arms.

Two days later, just before dawn, Jean-Charles arrives in their front yard with a bottle of wine from Louisbourg, to the delight of the "priest" Pétard. They prepare for the ceremony that will take place at sunrise, a sacred time in Mi'kmaw culture.

Rosalie is inside, helping Prémélia with her wedding dress.

"If only we had a mirror so you could see how beautiful you are," gushes Rosalie. "You look like a French princess…although I've never seen one."

"Thank you, but I doubt French princesses wear moccasins on their feet," answers the bride, smiling.

Having been clothed in rags and animal skins for years, Prémélia feels very strange dressed in such an elegant and extravagant dress. And she can hardly believe that she is about to marry the handsome and gallant man she has longed for.

In the first rays of sunlight over the valley, Jean-Charles, in his formal travelling attire, and Pétard, in the only clothes he owns, wait for Prémélia and Rosalie to join them. When the women arrive, Prémélia and Jean-Charles stand together and face the old couple.

"Jacques and Marie would be very happy to witness their little Prémélia's marriage to this honourable young man. I believe that Fidèle would also approve of his sister's choice. God bless this union. Welcome to the family, Jean-Charles à Violette!"

Pétard blesses their union in the Mi'kmaw language to honour the deceased parents of the groom. The newlyweds and the old couple kiss as the morning sun reflects their great joy, mixed with a little sadness for not having shared this day with the rest of their family.

# The Yellow Warbler

*Twelve years pass. In 1775 the Memramkouke region is, for the* time being, a safe haven for Acadian families. Many have been released from prisons in the English forts. A few more have come from the woods, and some have returned from the Thirteen Colonies and New France.

The rich Acadian farmland has been given to British officers and newly arrived English colonists. Upon seeing their farmland, and, in some rare cases, their homes, inhabited by the English, the Acadians' heartbreak is almost unbearable. Will they be able to stay in Acadie? Will their loved ones make it back?

Even in Memramkouke, the future is uncertain. Nevertheless, having no place to go, Acadians stay and maintain the dykes for the new "landowners." The Acadians work very hard to rebuild aboiteaux, levées, homes, and barns. They pray to stay and live in peace.

La Butte-à-Pétard is now part of le Village-des-Piau, due to the arrival of Piau Belliveau's large family, whose farmland in the Annapolis Valley was given to New England Planters. Pétard's family is also growing larger: Jean-Charles and Prémélia have welcomed six children.

One day during planting season, some of Prémélia's children are busy planting potatoes on la Butte. The older boys help Jean-Charles and the men of the village build a new levée. In the family home, near the hearth, Pétard and Rosalie are each rocking a baby.

"Ti-Pruce came by when you were in the marsh," says Rosalie. "He told me that a small group of Acadians will soon be passing through. Some of them insist on returning to their farms in Grand-Pré. They'll have to learn for themselves that no Acadian will be welcome there.

"Where are they coming from?"

"Apparently, they spent twenty years in Must-achoo-sets."

"Cla! Cla! You mean Massachusetts. Did he have news of the rebellion in the English colonies?"

"It's a real war now. The Acadians there will be caught once again between two fires—only this time, between the British and their own English colonists."

"Who would've thought that in such a short time the Redcoats would be fighting their own? They must like to fight. It doesn't surprise me now that the Redcoats and Bluecoats didn't believe that Acadians would remain neutral. Don't worry about our people. It'll be easier for them to flee to Acadie; the authorities will be preoccupied with their latest war."

"But Pétard, the forest is still full of dangers, and the cold and hunger will kill some of the Acadians. They're already weak from their wretched exile."

"That's right, Rosalie. Some will die on the journey, but I believe a good number will survive. We did. Acadians are a sturdy lot. Let us pray for Jacques, Marie, Fidèle, and the child to be among them."

"Oh, how good it would be to finally have them with us on la Butte. Then we can die in peace!"

Prémélia walks in the door and overhears Rosalie.

"Mémère Rosalie, you're not talking about dying again?" she gently reprimands.

"Don't listen to me rattle on about Ti-Pruce's news. When will Jean-Charles and the boys be coming back?"

"They're going to work until dusk. They want to be ready for the landlord's inspection tomorrow." Prémélia sits her pail down on the table while keeping an eye on the window.

"That's odd. A yellow bird has been perched near the well for the last while, as if it's watching our home."

Rosalie and Pétard lay the sleeping babies in their cradles and join Prémélia at the window. Pétard remarks, "A yellow warbler. A large one. It's early in the season for it to be in these parts."

To their astonishment, the bird flies to the doorstep. Prémélia murmurs, "The refoul is coming." She walks over to the door and carefully opens it.

"Saint Esprit!" gasps Rosalie as the apparition of the bouhine fills the doorway.

They stand near the open door, astounded by a serene spirit magnificently cloaked in brilliant yellow warbler feathers. Gracefully, the bouhine opens her long, feathered cape, revealing a simple leather tunic. Around her neck is a leather string holding a small pouch with multicoloured feathers. She looks at Pétard with her deep black eyes and slowly nods, as if giving a silent thank you. The spirit becomes more and more luminescent, only to fade away before their very eyes.

"Sapristi! It's her!"

"Who is she, Pépère?"

"The Mi'kmaw I buried at la Pointe Rocheuse when I was a young."

They know the story well. Pétard has told it many times.

In the early days of Memramkouke's colonization by Acadians, Pétard had found the drowned body of a Mi'kmaw woman on the shore of la Pointe Rocheuse. Inside her feathered pouch were delicate bird bones and more feathers. Pétard assumed that her people had moved to another camp, so he buried the poor woman himself. With respect to Indigenous customs, he carried her to the Mi'kmaw campsite, where he dug a round hole. Following their tradition, he covered the side and bottom of the hole with cedar branches. He then placed the deceased on her knees, facing east. To help identify the Mi'kmaw woman, he planted a cross of sticks on which he tied a feather and bone taken from the pouch. When the Mi'kmaq returned to their camp, they said that no one was missing from their group. The identity of the drowned woman remained a mystery.

"Now I know the poor woman I buried was a bouhine."

"Saint Esprit!" exclaims Rosalie again in disbelief.

"Pépère, she's been like a guardian angel for our family. She saved us from the soldiers, and brought us to Kitpou when he was shot. I wonder…."

Prémélia goes back to the window and sees a man walking toward la Butte. He starts to walk faster and faster until he is running up to their house. Prémélia bolts out the door.

"Lia!" the man yells.

There is only one person who ever called her "Lia."

"Fidèle!" Prémélia cries, running to her brother.

They hold each other fiercely, tears streaming from their eyes. Fidèle sees his grandfather hobbling toward them.

"Pépère!"

"Fidèle! Oh, my Fidèle," wails Pétard. "You've grown up to be a big man like your father. I knew you would come back to us. Ah, Fidèle. You were always the most stubborn of all Pétards."

The three of them hold each other until their laughter and tears subside. Rosalie waits silently in the doorway, wiping her eyes with a corner of her apron.

"Grandson, Rosalie is now a Pétard, too."

Fidèle walks over to hug the old woman and whispers, "Another stubborn one."

"Did you find Maman, Papa, and the baby?" asks Prémélia, anxiously.

"Maman and our sister Jacqueline have been living in Louisiana. It took me a long time to find Papa. He was in San Domingue, where he had been suffering from yellow fever. They didn't know if any of us were still alive. Fortunately, neither of our parents remarried. They never gave up on their dream of coming back to Acadie. Our parents are on board a ship from Boston and will be here in a week!"

"A week! Our prayers are answered! Oh, Fidèle," says Prémélia, hugging her brother again.

"What? Bluecoats are bringing Acadians home?" asks Pétard, stunned. "Fidèle, how could you trust them, after all they did to us!"

"Saint Esprit!" Rosalie says, shaking her head.

"Pépère, they're doing it for me in recognition of my service. Fighting for the Bluecoats against the British was the best way for me to get our family back together."

"Sapristi, Fidèle! The Bluecoats!" repeats Pétard, incredulous.

"And our sister? She's with our parents?"

"No, Lia. Jacqueline is almost twenty years old

and looks just like you except for her brown eyes. She chose to stay in Louisiana with her husband, a good Acadian man from Île Saint-Jean. She's very much loved by her husband's big family. They have a prosperous farm near the Beausoleils. Still, it was very difficult for Maman and Jacqueline to say goodbye. But they knew that Maman would be happier with Papa and the rest of the family in Acadie."

"Beausoleil ended up in Louisiana?"

"Yes, Pépère. He and his brother died of yellow fever a year after their arrival. Beausoleil was a hero to many Acadians."

"Little brother, you're our hero."

"You're my heroes, you stubborn lot…and Kitpou was too. I heard of his death when I was with Beausoleil. So many Mi'kmaq and Acadians have died. So many Acadians can't return to Acadie. Yet, here you are! I always knew that you would be."

"And with Prémélia, your brother-in-law, Jean-Charles—"

"Not Jean-Charles à Violette!" blurts Fidèle, happily.

Pétard continues, "and their six stubborn children—"

"Six!" shouts Fidèle, overjoyed.

His grandfather concludes, "—there will be Pétards slurping fricot on their hill for awhile yet! Cla! Cla! Cla!"

# Glossary

*Aboiteaux*: sluice gates

*Adieu:* goodbye

*amoureux*: lovers

*bénaise*: old French word for happy

*bouhine (puoin)*: in the Mi'kmaw language, a Mi'kmaw man or woman with supernatural powers

*butte*: hill

*capine*: large cotton bonnet worn by Acadian women and girls

*cher (mon)* or *chère (ma)*: my dear

*enfilée*: ball of worms used for fishing tommy cod

*escrable*: rascals in Acadian French

*fricot*: Acadian soup made with poultry or rabbit, seasoned with summer savory

*Grand Dérangement*: great displacement or great upheaval, a term used by Acadians for their deportation and the years surrounding that period

*Great Snows*: Mi'kmaw term for February

*la butte*: the hill

*levée*: levee or dyke

*ma belle* : my beauty

*madouesse*: porcupine in the Mi'kmaw language

*mashcoui*: birchbark

*mon Dieu*: my God

*nigog*: Mi'kmaw word for a fishing trident

*passe-pierre*: goose tongue greens

*Partons la mer est belle*: Let's leave, the sea is beautiful; also the title of a popular old French song

*Petit (mon)* or *petite (ma)*: my little one

*poulamon*: Mi'kmaw word still used by Acadians for tommy cod

*refoul*: tidal bore

*Saint Esprit*: Holy Spirit

*Sapristi*: For God's sake, good grief

*Tintamarre*: sound made by a flock of ducks in a marsh, loud noises

# PLACE NAMES

This book uses old Acadian place names. Below are their equivalents.

Chipoudie Bay: Shepody Bay

Baie Française: Bay of Fundy

New France: Québec

Île Saint-Jean: Prince Edward Island

Île Royale: Cape Breton

Beaubassin: Amherst

Le Coude: Moncton

Cap des Demoiselles: Hopewell Rocks

San Domingue: Haiti

Pierre à Michel: Belliveau Village

Pointe-à-Boulots: Upper Dorchester

Petcoudiac: Petitcodiac

Memramkouke: Memramcook